THE GOLDEN SCARECROW

HUGH WALPOLE

1st WORLD
LIBRARY
Literary Society

The Golden Scarecrow

Hugh Walpole

© 1st World Library, 2006
PO Box 2211
Fairfield, IA 52556
www.1stworldlibrary.com
First Edition

LCCN: 2006937828

Softcover ISBN: 978-1-4218-3352-1
Hardcover ISBN: 978-1-4218-3252-4
eBook ISBN: 978-1-4218-3452-8

Purchase *"The Golden Scarecrow"*
as a traditional bound book at:
www.1stWorldLibrary.com/purchase.asp?ISBN=978-1-4218-3352-1

1ˢᵗ World Library Literary Society

Giving Back to the World

"If you want to work on the core problem, it's early school literacy."

- James Barksdale, former CEO of Netscape

"No skill is more crucial to the future of a child, or to a democratic and prosperous society, than literacy."

- Los Angeles Times

Literacy... means far more than learning how to read and write... The aim is to transmit... knowledge and promote social participation."

- UNESCO

"Literacy is not a luxury, it is a right and a responsibility. If our world is to meet the challenges of the twenty-first century we must harness the energy and creativity of all our citizens."

- President Bill Clinton

"Parents should be encouraged to read to their children, and teachers should be equipped with all available techniques for teaching literacy, so the varying needs and capacities of individual kids can be taken into account."

- Hugh Mackay

CONTENTS

PROLOGUE

HUGH SEYMOUR

I

When Hugh Seymour was nine years of age he was sent from Ceylon, where his parents lived, to be educated in England. His relations having, for the most part, settled in foreign countries, he spent his holidays as a very minute and pale-faced "paying guest" in various houses where other children were of more importance than he, or where children as a race were of no importance at all. It was in this way that he became during certain months of 1889 and 1890 and '91 a resident in the family of the Rev. William Lasher, Vicar of Clinton St. Mary, that large rambling village on the edge of Roche St. Mary Moor in South Glebeshire.

He spent there the two Christmases of 1890 and 1891 (when he was ten and eleven years of age), and it is with the second of these that the following incident, and indeed the whole of this book, has to do. Hugh Seymour could not, at the period of which I write, be called an attractive child; he was not even "interesting" or "unusual." He was very minutely made, with bones so brittle that it seemed that, at any moment, he might crack and splinter into sharp little pieces; and I am afraid that no one would have minded very greatly had this occurred. But although, he was so thin his face had a white and overhanging appearance, his cheeks being pale and puffy and his under-lip jutted forward in front of projecting teeth—he was known as the "White Rabbit" by his schoolfellows. He was not, however, so ugly as this appearance would apparently convey, for his large, grey eyes, soft and even, at times agreeably humorous, were pleasant and cheerful.

During these years when he knew Mr. Lasher he was undoubtedly unfortunate. He was shortsighted, but no one had, as yet, discovered this, and he was, therefore, blamed for much clumsiness that he could not prevent and for a good deal of sensitiveness that came quite simply from his eagerness to do what he was told and his inability to see his way to do it. He was not, at this time, easy with strangers and seemed to them both conceited and awkward. Conceit was far from him—he was, in fact, amazed at so feeble a creature as himself!—but awkward he was, and very often greedy, selfish, impetuous, untruthful and even cruel: he was nearly always dirty, and attributed this to the evil wishes of some malign fairy who flung mud upon him, dropped him into puddles and covered him with ink simply for the fun of the thing!

He did not, at this time, care very greatly for reading; he told himself stories—long stories with enormous families in them, trains of elephants, ropes and ropes of pearls, towers of ivory, peacocks, and strange meals of saffron buns, roast chicken, and gingerbread. His active, everyday concern, however, was to become a sportsman; he wished to be the best cricketer, the best footballer, the fastest runner of his school, and he had not—even then faintly he knew it—the remotest chance of doing any of these things even moderately well. He was bullied at school until his appointment as his dormitory's story-teller gave him a certain status, but his efforts at cricket and football were mocked with jeers and insults. He could not throw a cricket-ball, he could not see to catch one after it was thrown to him, did he try to kick a football he missed it, and when he had run for five minutes he saw purple skies and silver stars and has cramp in his legs. He had, however, during these years at Mr. Lasher's, this great over mastering ambition.

In his sleep, at any rate, he was a hero; in the wide-awake

world he was, in the opinion of almost every one, a fool. He was exactly the type of boy whom the Rev. William Lasher could least easily understand. Mr. Lasher was tall and thin (his knees often cracked with a terrifying noise), blue-black about the cheeks hooked as to the nose, bald and shining as to the head, genial as to the manner, and practical to the shining tips of his fingers. He has not, at Cambridge, obtained a rowing blue, but "had it not been for a most unfortunate attack of scarlet fever—" He was President of the Clinton St. Mary Cricket Club, 1890 (matches played, six; lost, five; drawn, one) knew how to slash the ball across the net at a tennis garden party, always read the prayers in church as though he were imploring God to keep a straighter bat and improve His cut to leg, and had a passion for knocking nails into walls, screwing locks into doors, and making chicken runs. He was, he often thanked his stars, a practical Realist, and his wife, who was fat, stupid, and in a state of perpetual wonder, used to say of him, "If Will hadn't been a clergyman he would have made *such* an engineer. If God had blessed us with a boy, I'm sure he would have been something scientific. Will's no dreamer." Mr Lasher was kindly of heart so long as you allowed him to maintain that the world was made for one type of humanity only. He was as breezy as a west wind, loved to bathe in the garden pond on Christmas Day ("had to break the ice that morning"), and at penny readings at the village schoolroom would read extracts from "Pickwick," and would laugh so heartily himself that he would have to stop and wipe his eyes. "If you must read novels," he would say, "read Dickens. Nothing to offend the youngest among us—fine breezy stuff with an optimism that does you good and people you get to know and be fond of. By Jove, I can still cry over Little Nell and am not ashamed of it."

He had the heartiest contempt for "wasters" and "failures," and he was afraid there were a great many in the world. "Give me a man who is a man," he would say, "a man who can hit a ball for six, run ten miles before breakfast and take his knocks with the best of them. Wasn't it Browning who said,

"God's in His heaven,
All's right with the world."

Browning was a great teacher—after Tennyson, one of our greatest. Where are such men to-day!"

He was, therefore, in spite of his love for outdoor pursuits, a cultured man.

It was natural, perhaps, that he should find Hugh Seymour "a pity." Nearly everything that he said about Hugh Seymour began with the words—

"It's a pity that—"

"It's a pity that you can't get some red into your cheeks, my boy."

"It's a pity you don't care about porridge. You must learn to like it."

"It's a pity you can't even make a little progress with your mathematics."

"It's a pity you told me a lie because—"

"It's a pity you were rude to Mrs. Lasher. No gentleman—"

"It's a pity you weren't attending when—"

Mr. Lasher was, very earnestly, determined to do his best for the boy, and, as he said, "You see, Hugh, if we do our best for you, you must do your best for us. Now I can't, I'm afraid, call this your best."

Hugh would have liked to say that it *was* the best that he could do in that particular direction (very probably Euclid), but if only he might be allowed to try his hand in quite *another* direction, he might do something very fine indeed. He never, of course, had a chance of saying this, nor would such a declaration have greatly benefited him, because, for Mr. Lasher, there was only one way for every one and the sooner (if you were a small boy) you followed it the better.

"Don't dream, Hugh," said Mr. Lasher, "remember that no man ever did good-work by dreaming. The goal is to the strong. Remember that."

Hugh, did remember it and would have liked very much to be as strong as possible, but whenever he tried feats of strength he failed and looked foolish.

"My dear boy, *that's* not the way to do it," said Mr. Lasher; "it's a pity that you don't listen to what I tell you."

II

A very remarkable fact about Mr. Lasher was this—that he paid no attention whatever to the county in which he lived. Now there are certain counties in England where it is possible to say, "I am in England," and to leave it at that; their quality is simply English with no more individual personality. But Glebeshire has such an individuality, whether for good or evil, that it forces comment from the most sluggish and inattentive of human beings. Mr. Lasher was perhaps the only soul, living or dead, who succeeded in living in it during forty years (he is still there, he is a Canon now in Polchester) and never saying anything about it. When on his visits to London people inquired his opinion of Glebeshire, he would say: "Ah well!... I'm afraid Methodism and intemperance are very strong ... all the same, we're fighting 'em, fighting 'em!"

This was the more remarkable in that Mr. Lasher lived upon the very edge of Roche St. Mary Moor, a stretch of moor and sand. Roche St. Mary Moor, that runs to the sea, contains the ruins of St. Arthe Church (buried until lately in the sand, but recently excavated through the kind generosity of Sir John

Porthcullis, of Borhaze, and shown to visitors, 6d. a head, Wednesday and Saturday afternoons free), and in one of the most romantic, mist-laden, moon-silvered, tempest-driven spots in the whole of Great Britain.

The road that ran from Clinton St. Mary to Borhaze across the moor was certainly a wild, rambling, beautiful affair, and when the sea-mists swept across it and the wind carried the cry of the Bell of Trezent Rock in and out above and below, you had a strange and moving experience. Mr. Lasher was certainly compelled to ride on his bicycle from Clinton St. Mary to Borhaze and back again, and never thought it either strange or moving. "Only ten at the Bible meeting to-night. Borhaze wants waking up. We'll see what open-air services can do." What the moor thought about Mr. Lasher it is impossible to know!

Hugh Seymour thought about the moor continually, but he was afraid to mention his ideas of it in public. There was a legend in the village that several hundred years ago some pirates, driven by storm into Borhaze, found their way on to the moor and, caught by the mist, perished there; they are to be seen, says the village, in powdered wigs, red coats, gold lace, and swords, haunting the sand-dunes. God help the poor soul who may fall into their hands! This was a very pleasant story, and Hugh Seymour's thoughts often crept around and about it. He would like to find a pirate, to bring him to the vicarage, and present him to Mr. Lasher. He knew that Mrs. Lasher would say, "Fancy, a pirate. Well! now, fancy! Well, here's a pirate!" And that Mr. Lasher would say, "It's a pity, Hugh, that you don't choose your company more carefully. Look at the man's nose!"

Hugh, although he was only eleven, knew this. Hugh did on one occasion mention the pirates. "Dreaming again, Hugh! Pity they fill your head with such nonsense! If they read their Bibles more!"

Nevertheless, Hugh continued his dreaming. He dreamt of the

moor, of the pirates, of the cobbled street in Borhaze, of the cry of the Trezent Bell, of the deep lanes and the smell of the flowers in them, of making five hundred not out at cricket, of doing a problem in Euclid to Mr. Lasher's satisfaction, of having a collar at the end of the week as clean as it had been at the beginning, of discovering the way to make a straight parting in the hair, of not wriggling in bed when Mrs. Lasher kissed him at night, of many, many other things.

He was at this time a very lonely boy. Until Mr. Pidgen paid his visit he was most remarkably lonely. After that visit he was never lonely again.

III

Mr. Pidgen came on a visit to the vicarage three days before Christmas. Hugh Seymour saw him first from the garden. Mr. Pidgen was standing at the window of Mr. Lasher's study; he was staring in front of him at the sheets of light that flashed and darkened and flashed again across the lawn, at the green cluster of holly-berries by the drive-gate, at the few flakes of snow that fell, lazily, carelessly, as though they were trying to decide whether they would make a grand affair of it or not, and perhaps at the small, grubby boy who was looking at him with one eye and trying to learn the Collect for the day (it was Sunday) with the other. Hugh had never before seen any one in the least like Mr. Pidgen. He was short and round, and his head was covered with tight little curls. His cheeks were chubby and red and his nose small, his mouth also very small. He had no chin. He was wearing a bright blue velvet waistcoat with brass buttons, and over his black shoes there shone white spats.

Hugh had never seen white spats before. Mr. Pidgen shone with cleanliness, and he had supremely the air of having been exactly as he was, all in one piece, years ago. He was like one of the china ornaments in Mrs. Lasher's drawing-room that the housemaid is told to be so careful about, and concerning whose destruction Hugh heard her on at least one occasion declaring, in a voice half tears, half defiance, "Please, ma'am, it wasn't me. It just slipped of itself!" Mr. Pidgen would break very completely were he dropped.

The first thing about him that struck Hugh was his amazing difference from Mr. Lasher. It seemed strange that any two people so different could be in the same house. Mr. Lasher never gleamed or shone, he would not break with however violent an action you dropped him, he would certainly never wear white spats.

Hugh liked Mr. Pidgen at once. They spoke for the first time at the mid-day meal, when Mr. Lasher said, "More Yorkshire pudding, Pidgen?" and Mr. Pidgen said, "I adore it."

Now Yorkshire pudding happened to be one of Hugh's special passions just then, particularly when it was very brown and crinkly, so he said quite spontaneously and without taking thought, as he was always told to do,

"So do I!"

"My *dear* Hugh!" said Mrs. Lasher; "how very greedy! Fancy! After all you've been told! Well, well! Manners, manners!"

"I don't know," said Mr. Pidgen (his mouth was full). "I said it first, and I'm older than he is. I should know better.... I like boys to be greedy, it's a good sign—a good sign. Besides. Sunday—after a sermon—one naturally feels a bit peckish. Good enough sermon, Lasher, but a bit long."

Mr. Lasher of course did not like this, and, indeed, it was evident to any one (even to a small boy) that the two gentlemen would have different opinions upon every possible subject. However, Hugh loved Mr. Pidgen there and then, and decided that he would put him into the story then running (appearing in nightly numbers from the moment of his departure to bed to the instant of slumber—say ten minutes);

he would also, in the imaginary cricket matches that he worked out on paper, give Mr. Pidgen an innings of two hundred not out and make him captain of Kent. He now observed the vision very carefully and discovered several strange items in his general behaviour. Mr. Pidgen was fond of whistling and humming to himself; he was restless and would walk up and down a room with his head in the air and his hands behind his broad back, humming (out of tune) "Sally in our Alley," or "Drink to me only." Of course this amazed Mr. Lasher.

He would quite suddenly stop, stand like a top spinning, balanced on his toes, and cry, "Ah! Now I've got it! No, I haven't! Yes, I have. By God, it's gone again!"

To this also Mr. Lasher strongly objected, and Hugh heard him say, "Really, Pidgen, think of the boy! Think of the boy!" and Mr. Pidgen exclaimed, "By God, so I should!... Beg pardon, Lasher! Won't do it again! Lord save me, I'm a careless old drunkard!" He had any number of strange phrases that were new and brilliant and exciting to the boy, who listened to him. He would say, "by the martyrs of Ephesus!" or "Sunshine and thunder!" or "God stir your slumbers!" when he thought any one very stupid. He said this last one day to Mrs. Lasher, and of course she was very much astonished. She did not from the first like him at all. Mr. Pidgen and Mr. Lasher had been friends at Cambridge and had not met one another since, and every one knows that that is a dangerous basis for the renewal of friendship. They had a little dispute on the very afternoon of Mr. Pidgen's arrival, when Mr. Lasher asked his guest whether he played golf.

"God preserve my soul! No!" said Mr. Pidgen. Mr. Lasher then explained that playing golf made one thin, hungry and self-restrained. Mr. Pidgen said that he did not wish to be the first or last of these, and that he was always the second, and that golf was turning the fair places of England into troughs for the moneyed pigs of the Stock Exchange to swill in.

"My dear Pidgen!" cried Mr. Lasher, "I'm afraid no one could call me a moneyed pig with any justice—more's the pity—and a game of golf to me is—"

"Ah! you're a parson, Lasher," said his guest.

In fact, by the evening of the second day of the visit it was obvious that Clinton St. Mary Vicarage might, very possibly, witness a disturbed Christmas. It was all very tiresome for poor Mrs. Lasher. On the late afternoon of Christmas Eve, Hugh heard the stormy conversation that follows—a conversation that altered the colour and texture of his after-life as such things may, when one is still a child.

IV

Christmas Eve was always, to Hugh, a day with glamour. He did not any longer hang up his stocking (although he would greatly have liked to do so), but, all day, his heart beat thickly at the thought of the morrow, at the thought of something more than the giving and receiving of presents, something more than the eating of food, something more than singing hymns that were delightfully familiar, something more than putting holly over the pictures and hanging mistletoe on to the lamp in the hall. Something there was in the day like going home, like meeting people again whom one had loved once, and not seen for many years, something as warm and romantic and lightly coloured *and* as comforting as the most inspired and impossible story that one could ever, lying in bed and waiting for sleep, invent.

To-day there was no snow but a frost, and there was a long bar of saffron below the cold sky and a round red ball of a sun. Hugh was sitting in a corner of Mr. Lasher's study, looking at Doré's "Don Quixote," when the two gentlemen came in. He was sitting in a dark corner and they, because they were angry with one another, did not recognise any one except themselves. Mr. Lasher pulled furiously at his pipe and Mr. Pidgen stood up by the fire with his short fat legs spread wide and his mouth

Hugh Walpole

smiling, but his eyes vexed and rather indignant.

"My dear Pidgen," said Mr. Lasher, "you misunderstand me, you do indeed! It may be (I would be the first to admit that, like most men, I have my weakness) that I lay too much stress upon the healthy, physical, normal life, upon seeing things as they are and not as one would like to see them to be. I don't believe that dreaming ever did any good to any man!"

"It's only produced some of the finest literature the world has ever known," said Mr. Pidgen.

"Ah! Genius! If you or I were geniuses, Pidgen, that would be another affair. But we're not; we're plain, common-place humdrum human beings with souls to be saved and work to do—work to do!"

There was a little pause after that, and Hugh, looking at Mr. Pidgen, saw the hurt look in his eyes deepen.

"Come now, Lasher," he said at last. "Let's be honest one with another; that's your line, and you say it ought to be mine. Come now, as man to man, you think me a damnable failure now—beg pardon—complete failure—don't you? Don't be afraid of hurting me. I want to know!"

Mr. Lasher was really a kindly man, and when his eyes beheld things—there were of course many things that they never beheld—he would do his best to help anybody. He wanted to help Mr. Pidgen now; but he was also a truthful man.

"My dear Pidgen! Ha, ha! What a question! I'm sure many, many people enjoy your books immensely. I'm sure they do, oh, yes!"

"Come, now, Lasher, the truth. You won't hurt my feelings. If you were discussing me with a third person you'd say, wouldn't you? 'Ah, poor Pidgen might have done something if he hadn't let his fancy run away with him. I was with him at

Cambridge. He promised well, but I'm afraid one must admit that he's failed—he would never stick to anything.'"

Now this was so exactly what Mr. Lasher had, on several occasions, said about his friend that he was really for the moment at a loss. He pulled at his pipe, looked very grave, and then said:

"My dear Pidgen, you must remember our lives have followed such different courses. I can only give you my point of view. I don't myself care greatly for romances—fairy tales and so on. It seems to me that for a grown-up man.... However, I don't pretend to be a literary fellow; I have other work, other duties, picturesque, but nevertheless necessary."

"Ah!" exclaimed Mr. Pidgen, who, considering that he had invited his host's honest opinion, should not have become irritated because he had obtained it; "that's just it. You people all think only *you* know what is necessary. Why shouldn't a fairy story be as necessary as a sermon? A lot more necessary, I dare say. You think you're the only people who can know anything about it. You people never use your imaginations."

"Nevertheless," said Mr. Lasher, very bitterly (for he had always said, "If one does not bring one's imagination into one's work one's work is of no value"), "writers of idle tales are not the only people who use their imaginations. And, if you will allow me, without offence, to say so, Pidgen, your books, even amongst other things of the same sort, have not been the most successful."

This remark seemed to pour water upon all the anger in Mr. Pidgen's heart. His eyes expressed scorn, but not now for Mr. Lasher—for himself. His whole figure drooped and was bowed like a robin in a thunderstorm.

"That's true enough. Bless my soul, Lasher, that's true enough. They hardly sell at all. I've written a dozen of them now, 'The Blue Pouncet Box,' 'The Three-tailed Griffin,' 'The Tree without any Branches,' but you won't want to be bothered with the names of them. 'The Griffin' went into two editions, but it was only because the pictures were rather sentimental. I've often said to myself, 'If a thing doesn't sell in these days it must be good,' but I've not really convinced myself. I'd like them to have sold. Always, until now, I've had hopes of the next one, and thought that it would turn out better, like a woman with her babies. I seem to have given up expecting that now. It isn't, you know, being always hard-up that I mind so much, although that, mind you, isn't pleasant, no, by Jehoshaphat, it isn't. But we would like now and again to find that other people have enjoyed what one hoped they *would* enjoy. But I don't know, they always seem too old for children and too young for grown-ups—my stories, I mean."

It was one of the hardest traits in Mr. Lasher's character, as Hugh well realised, "to rub it in" over a fallen foe. He considered this his duty; it was also, I am afraid, a pleasure. "It's a pity," he said, "that things should not have gone better; but there are so many writers to-day that I wonder any one writes at all. We live in a practical, realistic age. The leaders amongst us have decided that every man must gird his loins and go out to fight his battles with real weapons in a real cause, not sit dreaming at his windows looking down upon the busy market-place." (Mr. Lasher loved what he called "images." There were many in his sermons.) "But, my dear Pidgen, it is in no way too late. Give up your fairy stories now that they have been proved a failure."

Here Mr. Pidgen, in the most astonishing way, was suddenly in a terrible temper. "They're not!" he almost screamed. "Not at all. Failures, from the worldly point of view, yes; but there are some who understand. I would not have done anything else if I could. You, Lasher, with your soup-tickets and your choir-treats, think there's no room for me and my fairy stories. I tell you, you may find yourself jolly well mistaken one of these days. Yes, by Cæsar, you may. How do you know what's best worth doing? If you'd listened a little more to the things you were told when you were a baby, you'd be a more intelligent man now."

"When I was a baby," said Mr. Lasher, incredulously, as though that were a thing that he never possibly could have been, "my *dear* Pidgen!"

"Ah, you think it absurd," said the other, a little cooler again. "But how do you know who watched over your early years and wanted you to be a dreamy, fairy tale kind of person instead of the cayenne pepper sort of man you are. There's always some one there, I tell you, and you can have your choice, whether you'll believe more than you see all your life or less than you see. Every baby knows about it; then, as they grow older, it fades and, with many people, goes altogether. He's never left *me*, St. Christopher, you know, and that's one thing. Of course, the ideal thing is somewhere between the two; recognise St. Christopher and see the real world as well. I'm afraid neither you nor I is the ideal man, Lasher. Why, I tell you, any baby of three knows more than you do! You're proud of never seeing beyond your nose. I'm proud of never seeing my nose at all: we're both wrong. But I *am* ready to admit *your* uses. You *never* will admit mine; and it isn't any use your denying my Friend. He stayed with you a bit when you just arrived, but I expect he soon left you. You're jolly glad he did."

"My *dear* Pidgen," said Mr. Lasher, "I haven't understood a word."

Pidgen shook his head. "You're right. That's just what's the matter with me. I can't even put what I see plainly." He sighed deeply. "I've failed. There's no doubt about it. But, although I know that, I've had a happy life. That's the funny part of it. I've enjoyed it more than you ever will, Lasher. At least, I'm never lonely. I like my food, too, and one's head's always full of jolly ideas, if only they seemed jolly to other people."

"Upon my word, Pidgen," said Mr. Lasher. At this moment Mrs. Lasher opened the door.

Hugh Walpole

"Well, well. Fancy! Sitting over the fire talking! Oh, you men! Tea! tea! Tea, Will! Fancy talking all the afternoon! Well!"

No one had noticed Hugh. He, however, had understood Mr. Pidgen better than Mr. Lasher did.

V

This conversation aroused in Hugh, for various reasons, the greatest possible excitement. He would have liked to have asked Mr. Pidgen many questions. Christmas Day came, and a beautiful day enthroned it: a pale blue sky, faint and clear, was a background to misty little clouds that hovered, then fled and disappeared, and from these flakes of snow fell now and then across the shining sunlight. Early in the winter afternoon a moon like an orange feather sailed into the sky as the lower stretches of blue changed into saffron and gold. Trees and hills and woods were crystal-clear, and shone with an intensity of outline as though their shapes had been cut by some giant knife against the background. Although there was no wind the air was so expectant that the ringing of church bells and the echo of voices came as though across still water. The colour of the sunlight was caught in the cups and runnels of the stiff frozen roads and a horse's hoofs echoed, sharp and ringing, over fields and hedges. The ponds were silvered into a sheet of ice, so thin that the water showed dark beneath it. All the trees were rimmed with hoar-frost.

On Christmas afternoon, when three o'clock had just struck from the church tower, Hugh and Mr. Pidgen met, as though by some conspirator's agreement, by the garden gate. They had said nothing to one another and yet there they were; they both glanced anxiously back at the house and then Mr. Pidgen said:

"Suppose we take a walk."

"Thank you very much," said Hugh. "Tea isn't till half-past four."

"Very well, then, suppose you lead the way." They walked a little, and then Hugh said: "I was there yesterday, in the study, when you talked all that about your books, and everything." The words came from him in little breathless gusts because he was excited.

Mr. Pidgen stopped and looked upon him. "Thunder and sunshine! You don't say so! What under heaven were you doing?"

"I was reading, and you came in and then I was interested."

"Well?"

Hugh dropped his voice.

"I understood all that you meant. I'd like to read your books if I may. We haven't any in the house."

"Bless my soul! Here's some one wants to read my books!" Mr. Pidgen was undoubtedly pleased. "I'll send you some. I'll send you them all!"

Hugh gasped with pleasure. "I'll read them all, however many there are!" he said excitedly. "Every word."

"Well," said Mr. Pidgen, "that's more than any one else has ever done."

"I'd rather be with you," said the boy very confidently, "than Mr. Lasher. I'd rather write stories than preach sermons that no one wants to listen to." Then more timidly he continued: "I know what you meant about the man who comes when you're a baby. I remember him quite well, but I never can say anything because they'd say I was silly. Sometimes I think he's still hanging round only he doesn't come to the vicarage much. He doesn't like Mr. Lasher much, I expect. But I *do* remember him. He had a beard and I used to think it funny the nurse didn't see him. That was before we went to Ceylon, you know, we used to live in Polchester then. When it was nearly dark and not quite he'd be there. I forgot about him in Ceylon, but since I've been here I've wondered ... it's sometimes like some one whispering to you and you know if you turn round he won't be there, but he *is* there all the same. I made twenty-five last summer against Porthington Grammar; they're not much good *really*, and it was our second eleven, and I was nearly out second ball; anyway I made twenty-five, and afterwards as I was ragging about I suddenly thought of him. I *know* he was pleased. If it had been a little darker I believe I'd have seen him. And then last night, after I was in bed and was thinking about what you'd said I *know* he was near the window, only I didn't look lest he should go away. But of course Mr. Lasher would say that's all rot, like the pirates, only I *know* it isn't." Hugh broke off for lack of breath, nothing else would have stopped him. When he was encouraged he was a terrible talker. He suddenly added in a sharp little voice like the report from a pistol: "So one can't be lonely or anything, can one, if there's always some one about?"

Mr. Pidgen was greatly touched. He put his hand upon Hugh's shoulder. "My dear boy," he said, "my dear boy—dear me, dear me. I'm afraid you're going to have a dreadful time when you grow up. I really mustn't encourage you. And yet, who can help himself?"

"But you said yourself that you'd seen him, that you knew him quite well?"

"And so I do—and so I do. But you'll find, as you grow older, there are many people who won't believe you. And there's this, too. The more you live in your head, dreaming and seeing things that aren't there, the less you'll see the things that *are* there. You'll always be tumbling over things. You'll never get on. You'll never be a success."

"Never mind," said Hugh, "it doesn't matter much what you say now, you're only talking 'for my good' like Mr. Lasher. I don't care, I heard what you said yesterday, and it's made all the difference. I'll come and stay with you."

"Well, so you shall," said Mr. Pidgen. "I can't help it. You shall come as often as you like. Upon my soul, I'm younger to-day than I've felt for a long time. We'll go to the pantomime together if you aren't too old for it. I'll manage to ruin you all right. What's that shining?" He pointed in front of him.

They had come to a rise in the Polwint Road. To their right, running to the very foot of their path, was the moor. It stretched away, like a cloud, vague and indeterminate to the horizon. To their left a dark brown field rose in an ascending wave to a ridge that cut the sky, now crocus-coloured. The field was lit with the soft light of the setting sun. On the ridge of the field something, suspended, it seemed, in midair, was shining like a golden fire.

"What's that?" said Mr. Pidgen again. "It's hanging. What the devil!"

They stopped for a moment, then started across the field. When they had gone a little way Mr. Pidgen paused again.

"It's like a man with a golden helmet. He's got legs, he's coming to us."

They walked on again. Then Hugh cried, "Why, it's only an old Scarecrow. We might have guessed."

The sun, at that instant, sank behind the hills and the world was grey.

The Scarecrow, perched on the high ridge, waved its tattered sleeves in the air. It was an old tin can that had caught the light; the can hanging over the stake that supported it in drunken fashion seemed to wink at them. The shadows came streaming up from the sea and the dark woods below in the hollow drew closer to them.

The Scarecrow seemed to lament the departure of the light. "Here, mind," he said to the two of them, "you saw me in my glory just now and don't you forget it. I may be a knight in shining armour after all. It only depends upon the point of view."

"So it does," said Mr. Pidgen, taking his hat off, "you were very fine, I shan't forget."

VI

They stood there in silence for a time....

VII

At last they turned back and walked slowly home, the intimacy of their new friendship growing with their silence. Hugh was happier than he had ever been before. Behind the quiet evening light he saw wonderful prospects, a new life in which he might dream as he pleased, a new friend to whom he might tell these dreams, a new confidence in his own power....

But it was not to be.

That very night Mr. Pidgen died, very peacefully, in his sleep, from heart failure. He had had, as he had himself said, a happy life.

VIII

Years passed and Hugh Seymour grew up. I do not wish here to say much more about him. It happened that when he was twenty-four his work compelled him to live in that Square in London known as March Square (it will be very carefully described in a minute). Here he lived for five years, and, during that time, he was happy enough to gain the intimacy and confidence of some of the children who played in the Gardens there. They trusted him and told him more than they told many people. He had never forgotten Mr. Pidgen; that walk, that vision of the Scarecrow, stood, as such childish things will, for a landmark in his history. He came to believe that those experiences that he knew, in his own life, to be true, were true also for some others. That's as it may be. I can only say that Barbara and Angelina, Bim and even Sarah Trefusis were his friends. I daresay his theory is all wrong.

I can only say that I *know* that they were his friends; perhaps, after all, the Scarecrow *is* shining somewhere in golden armour. Perhaps, after all, one need not be so lonely as one often fancies that one is.

CHAPTER I

HENRY FITZGEORGE STRETHER

I

March Square is not very far from Hyde Park Corner in London Town. Behind the whir and rattle of the traffic it stands, spacious and cool and very old, muffled by the little streets that guard it, happily unconscious, you would suppose, that there were any in all the world so unfortunate as to have less than five thousand a year for their support. Perhaps a hundred years ago March Square might boast of such superior ignorance, but fashions change, to prevent, it may be, our own too easily irritated monotonies, and, for some time now, the Square has been compelled, here, there, in one corner and another, to admit the invader. It is true that the solemn, respectable grey house, No. 3, can boast that it is the town residence of His Grace the Duke of Crole and his beautiful young Duchess, née Miss Jane Tunster of New York City, but it is also true that No. — is in the possession of Mr. Munty Ross of Potted Shrimp fame, and there are Dr. Cruthen, the Misses Dent, Herbert Hoskins and his wife, whose incomes are certainly nearer to £500 than £5,000. Yes, rents and blue blood have come down in March Square; it is, certainly, not the less interesting for that, but—

Some of the houses can boast the days of good Queen Anne for their period. There is one, at the very corner where Somers Street turns off towards the Park, that was built only yesterday, and has about it some air of shame, a furtive embarrassment that it will lose very speedily. There is no house that can claim beauty, and yet the Square, as a whole, has a fine charm, something that age and colour, haphazard adventure, space and quiet have all helped towards.

There is, perhaps, no square in London that clings so tenaciously to any sign or symbol of old London that motor-cars and the increase of speed have not utterly destroyed. All the oldest London mendicants find their way, at different hours of the week, up and down the Square. There is, I believe, no other square in London where musicians are permitted. On Monday morning there is the blind man with the black patch over one eye; he has an organ (a very old one, with a painted picture of the Battle of Trafalgar on the front of it) and he wears an old black skull-cap. He wheezes out his old tunes (they are older than other tunes that March Square hears, and so, perhaps, March Square loves them). He goes despondently, and the tap of his stick sounds all the way round the Square. A small and dirty boy—his grandson, maybe—pushes the organ for him. On Tuesday there comes the remnants of a German band—remnants because now there are only the cornet, the flute and the trumpet. Sadly wind-blown, drunken and diseased they are, and the Square can remember when there were a number of them, hale and hearty young fellows, but drink and competition have been too strong for them. On Wednesdays there is sometimes a lady who sings ballads in a voice that can only be described as that contradiction in terms "a shrill contralto." Her notes are very piercing and can be heard from one end of the Square to the other. She sings "Annie Laurie" and "Robin Adair," and wears a battered hat of black straw. On Thursday there is a handsome Italian with a barrel organ that bears in its belly the very latest and most popular tunes. It is on Thursday that the Square learns the music of the moment; thus from one end of the year to the other does it keep pace with the movement.

On Fridays there is a lean and ragged man wearing large and, to the children of the Square, terrifying spectacles. He is a very gloomy fellow and sings hymn-tunes, "Rock of Ages," "There is a Happy Land," and "Jerusalem the Golden." On Saturdays there is a stout, happy little man with a harp. He has white hair and looks like a retired colonel. He cannot play the harp very much, but he is quite the most popular visitor of the week, and must be very rich indeed does he receive in other squares so handsome a reward for his melody as this one bestows; he is known as "Colonel Harry." In and out of these regular visitors there are, of course, many others. There is a dark, sinister man with a harmonium and a shivering monkey on a chain; there is an Italian woman, wearing bright wraps round her head, and she has a cage of birds who tell fortunes; there is a horsey, stable-bred, ferret-like man with, two performing dogs, and there is quite an old lady in a black bonnet and shawl who sings duets with her grand-daughter, a young thing of some fifty summers.

There can be nothing in the world more charming than the way the Square receives its friends. Let it number amongst its guests a Duchess, that is no reason why it should scorn "Colonel Harry" or "Mouldy Jim," the singer of hymns. Scorn, indeed, cannot be found within its grey walls, soft grey, soft green, soft white and blue—in these colours is the Square's body clothed, no anger in its mild eyes, nor contempt anywhere at its heart.

The Square is proud, and is proud with reason, of its garden. It is not a large garden as London gardens go. It has in its centre a fountain. Neptune, with a fine wreath of seaweed about his middle, blowing water through, his conch. There are two statues, the one of a general who fought in the Indian Mutiny and afterwards lived and died in the Square, the other of a mid-Victorian philanthropist whose stout figure and urbane self-satisfaction (as portrayed by the sculptor) bear witness to an easy conscience and an unimaginative mind. There is, round and about the fountain, a lovely green lawn, and there are many overhanging trees and shady corners. An air of peace the garden breathes, and that although children are for ever racing up and down it, shattering the stillness of the air with their cries, rivalling the bells of St. Matthew's round the corner with their piercing notes.

But it is the quality of the Square that nothing can take from it its peace, nothing temper its tranquillity. In the heat of the days motor-cars will rattle through, bells will ring, all the bustle of a frantic world invade its security; for a moment it submits, but in the evening hour, when the colours are being washed from the sky, and the moon, apricot-tinted, is rising slowly through the smoke, March Square sinks, with a little sigh, back into her peace again. The modern world has not yet touched her, nor ever shall.

II

The Duchess of Crole had three months ago a son, Henry Fitzgeorge, Marquis of Strether. Very fortunate that the first-born should be a son, very fortunate also that the first-born should be one of the healthiest, liveliest, merriest babies that it has ever been any one's good fortune to encounter. All smiles, chuckles and amiability is Henry Fitzgeorge; he is determined that all shall be well.

His birth was for a little time the sensation of the Square. Every one knew the beautiful Duchess; they had seen her drive, they had seen her walk, they had seen her in the picture-papers, at race-meetings and coming away from fashionable weddings. The word went round day by day as to his health; he was watched when he came out in his perambulator, and there was gossip as to his appearance and behaviour.

"A jolly little fellow."

"Just like his father."

"Rather early to say that, isn't it?"

"Well, I don't know, got the same smile. His mother's

Hugh Walpole

rather languid."

"Beautiful woman, though."

"Oh, lovely!"

Upon a certain afternoon in March about four o'clock, there was quite a gathering of persons in Henry Fitzgeorge's nursery. There was his mother, with those two great friends of hers, Lady Emily Blanchard and the Hon. Mrs. Vavasour; there was Her Grace's mother, Mrs. P. Tunster (an enormously stout lady); there was Miss Helen Crasper, who was staying in the house. These people were gathered at the end of the cot, and they looked down upon Henry Fitzgeorge, and he lay upon his back, gazed at them thoughtfully, and clenched and unclenched his fat hands.

Opposite his cot were some very wide windows, and three windows were filled with galleons of cloud—fat, bolster, swelling vessels, white, save where, in their curving sails, they had caught a faint radiance from the hidden sun. In fine procession, against the blue, they passed along. Very faint and muffled there came up from the Square the lingering notes of "Robin Adair." This is a Wednesday afternoon, and it is the lady with the black straw hat who is singing. The nursery has white walls—it is filled with colour; the fire blazes with a yellow-red gleam that rises and falls across the shining floor.

"I brought him a rattle, Jane, dear," said Mrs. Tunster, shaking in the air a thing of coral and silver. "He's got several, of course, but I guess you'll go a long way before you find anything cuter."

"It's too pretty," said Lady Emily.

"Too lovely," said the Hon. Mrs. Vavasour.

The Duchess looked down upon her son. "Isn't he old?" she said. "Thousands of years. You'd think he was laughing at the lot of us."

Mrs. Tunster shook her head. "Now don't you go imagining things, Jane, my dear. I used to be just like that, and your father would say, 'Now, Alice.'"

Her Grace raised her head. Her eyes were a little tired. She looked from her son to the clouds, and then back again to her son. She was remembering her own early days, the rich glowing colour of her own American country, the freedom, the space, the honesty.

"I guess you're tired, dear," said her mother. "With the party to-night and all. Why don't you go and rest a bit?"

"His eyes *are* old! He *does* despise us all."

Lady Emily, who believed in personal comfort and as little thinking as possible, put her arm through her friend's.

"Come along and give us some tea. He's a dear. Good-bye, you little darling. He *is* a pet. There, did you see him smiling? You *darling*. Tea I *must* have, Jane, dear—*at* once."

"You go on. I'm coming. Ring for it. Tell Hunter. I'll be with you in two minutes, mother."

Mrs. Tunster left her rattle in the nurse's hands. Then, with the two others, departed. Outside the nursery door she said in an American whisper:—"Jane isn't quite right yet. Went about a bit too soon. She's headstrong. She always has been. Doesn't do for her to think too much."

Her Grace was alone now with her son and heir and the nurse. She bent over the cot and smiled upon Henry Fitzgeorge; he smiled back at her, and even gave an absent-minded crow; but his gaze almost instantly swung back again to the window, through which, deeply and with solemn absorption, he watched the clouds.

She gave him her hand, and he closed his fingers about one of hers; but even that grasp was abstracted, as though he were not thinking of her at all, but was simply behaving like a gentleman.

"I don't believe he's realised me a bit, nurse," she said, turning away from the cot.

"Well, Your Grace, they always take time. It's early days."

"But what's he thinking of all the time?"

"Oh, just nothing, Your Grace."

"I don't believe it's nothing. He's trying to settle things. This—what it's all about—what he's got to do about it."

"It may be so, Your Grace. All babies are like that at first."

"His eyes are so old, so grave."

"He's a jolly little fellow, Your Grace."

"He's very little trouble, isn't he?"

"Less trouble than any baby I've ever had to do with. Got His Grace's happy temperament, if I may say so."

"Yes," the mother laughed. She crossed over to the window and looked down. "That poor woman singing down there. How awful! He'll be going down to Crole very shortly, Roberts. Splendid air for him there. But the Square's cheerful. He likes the garden, doesn't he?"

"Oh, yes, Your Grace; all the children and the fountain. But he's a happy baby. I should say he'd like anything."

For a moment longer she looked down into the Square. The discordant voice was giving "Annie Laurie" to the world.

"Good-bye, darling." She stepped forward, shook the silver and coral rattle. "See what grannie's given you!" She left it lying near his hand, and, with a little sigh, was gone.

III

Now, as the sun was setting, the clouds had broken into little pink bubbles, lying idly here and there upon the sky. Higher, near the top of the window, they were large pink cushions, three fat ones, lying sedately against the blue. During three months now Henry Fitzgeorge Strether had been confronted with the new scene, the new urgency on his part to respond to it. At first he had refused absolutely to make any response; behind him, around him, above him, below him, were still the old conditions; but they were the old conditions viewed, for some reason unknown to him, at a distance, and at a distance that was ever increasing. With every day something here in this new and preposterous world struck his attention, and with every fresh lure was he drawn more certainly from his old consciousness. At first he had simply rebelled; then, very slowly, his curiosity had begun to stir. It had stirred at first through food and touch; very pleasant this, very pleasant that.

Milk, sleep, light things that he could hold very tightly with his hands. Now, upon this March afternoon, he watched the pink clouds with a more intent gaze than he had given to them before. Their colour and shape bore some reference to the life that he had left. They were "like" a little to those other things. There, too, shadowed against the wall, was his Friend, his Friend, now the last link with everything that he knew.

At first, during the first week, he had demanded again and again to be taken back, and always he had been told to wait, to wait and see what was going to happen. So long as his Friend was there, he knew that he was not completely abandoned, and that this was only a temporary business, with its strange limiting circumstances, the way that one was tied and bound, the embarrassment of finding that all one's old means of

Hugh Walpole

communication were here useless. How desperate, indeed, would it have been had his Friend not been there, reassuring pervading him, surrounding him, always subduing those sudden inexplicable alarms.

He would demand: "When are we going to leave all this?"

"Wait. I know it seems absurd to you, but it's commanded you."

"Well, but—this is ridiculous. Where are all my old powers I Where are all the others?"

"You will understand everything one day. I'm afraid you're very uncomfortable. You will be less so as time passes. Indeed, very soon you will be very happy."

"Well, I'm doing my best to be cheerful. But you won't leave me?"

"Not so long as you want me."

"You'll stay until we go back again!"

"You'll never go back again."

"Never?"

"No."

Across the light the nurse advanced. She took him in her arms for a moment, turned his pillows, then layed him down again. As he settled down into comfort he saw his Friend, huge, a great shadow, mingling with the coloured lights of the flaming sky. All the world was lit, the white room glowed. A pleasant smell was in his nostrils.

"Where are all the others? They would like to share this pleasant moment, and I would warn them about the unpleasant ones."

"They are coming, some of them. I am with them as I am with you." Swinging across the Square were the evening bells of St. Matthew's.

Henry Fitzgeorge smiled, then chuckled, then dozed into a pleasant sleep.

IV

Asleep, awake, it had been for the most part the same to him. He swung easily, lazily upon the clouds; warmth and light surrounded him; a part of him, his toes, perhaps, would be suddenly cold, then he would cry, or he would strike his head against the side of his cot and it would hurt, and so then he would cry again. But these tears would not be tears of grief, but simply declarations of astonishment and wonder.

He did not, of course, realise that as, very slowly, very gradually he began to understand the terms and conditions of his new life, so with the same gradation, his Friend was expressed in those terms. Slowly that great shadow filled the room, took on human shape, until at last it would be only thus that he would appear. But Henry would not realise the change, soon he would not know that it had ever been otherwise. Dimly, out of chaos, the world was being made for him. There a square of colour, here something round and hard that was cool to touch, now a gleaming rod that ran high into the air, now a shape very soft and warm against which it was pleasant to lean. The clouds, the sweep of dim colour, the vast horizons of that other world yielded, day by day, to little concrete things—a patch of carpet, the leg of a chair, the shadow of the fire, clouds beyond the window, buttons on some one's clothes, the rails of his cot. Then there were voices, the touch of hands, some one's soft hair, some one who sang little songs to him.

He woke early one morning and realised the rattle that his grandmother had given to him. He suddenly realised it. He grasped the handle of it with his hand and found this cool and pleasant to touch. He then, by accident, made it tinkle, and instantly the prettiest noise replied to him. He shook it more lustily and the response was louder. He was, it seemed, master of this charming thing and could force it to do what he wished. He appealed to his Friend. Was not this a charming thing that he had found? He waved it and chuckled and crowed, and then his toes, sticking out beyond the bed-clothes, were nipped by the cold so that he halloed loudly. Perhaps the rattle had nipped his toes. He did not know, but he would cry because that eased his feelings.

That morning there came with his grandmother and mother a silly young woman who had, it was supposed, a great way with babies. "I adore babies," she said. "We understand one another in the most wonderful way."

Henry Fitzgeorge looked at her as she leaned over the cot and made faces at him. "Goo-goo-gum-goo," she cried.

"What is all this?" he asked his Friend. He laid down the rattle, and felt suddenly lonely and unhappy.

"Little pet—ug—la—la—goo—losh!" Henry Fitzgeorge raised his eyes. His Friend was a long, long way away; his eyes grew cold with contempt. He hated this thing that made the noises and closed out the light. He opened his eyes, he was about to burst into one of his most abandoned roars when his stare encountered his mother. Her eyes were watching him, and they had in them a glow and radiance that gave him a warm feeling of companionship. "I know," they seemed to say, "what you are thinking of. I agree with all that you are feeling about her. Only don't cry, she really isn't worth it." His mouth slowly closed then to thank her for her assistance, he raised the rattle and shook it at her. His eyes never left her face.

"Little darling," said the lady friend, but nevertheless

disappointed. "Lift him up, Jane. I'd like to see him in your arms."

But she shook her head. She moved away from the cot. Something so precious had been in that smile of her son's that she would not risk any rebuff.

Henry Fitzgeorge gave the strange lady one last look of disgust.

"If that comes again I'll bite it," he said to his Friend.

When these visitors had departed, he lay there remembering those eyes that had looked into his. All that day he remembered them, and it may be that his Friend, as he watched, sighed because the time for launching him had now come, that one more soul had passed from his sheltering arms out into the highroad of fine adventures. How easily they forget! How readily they forget! How eagerly they fling the pack of their old world from off their shoulders! He had seen, perhaps, so many go, thus lustily, upon their way, and then how many, at the end of it all, tired, worn, beaten to their very shadows, had he received at the end!

But it was so. This day was to see Henry Fitzgeorge's assertions of his independence. The hour when this life was to close, so definitely, so securely, the doors upon that other, had come. The shadow that had been so vast that it had filled the room, the Square, the world, was drawn now into small and human size.

Henry Fitzgeorge was never again to look so old.

V

As the fine, dim afternoon was closing, he was allowed, for half an hour before sleep, to sprawl upon the carpet in front of the fire. He had with him his rattle and a large bear which he stroked because it was comfortable; he had no personal feeling about it.

His mother came in.

"Let me have him for half an hour, nurse. Come back in half an hour's time."

The nurse left them.

Henry Fitzgeorge did not look at his mother.

He had the bear in his arms and was feeling it, and in his mind the warmth from the flickering, jumping flame and the soft, friendly submission of the fur beneath his fingers were part of the same mystery.

His mother had been motoring; her cheeks were flushed, and her dark clothes heightened, by their contrast, her colour. She knelt down on the carpet and then, with her hands folded on her lap, watched her son. He rolled the bear over and over, he poked it, he banged its head upon the ground. Then he was tired with it and took up the rattle. Then he was tired of that, and he looked across at his mother and chuckled.

His mind, however, was not at all concentrated upon her. He felt, on this afternoon, a new, a fresh interest in things. The carpet before him was a vast country and he did not propose to explore it, but sucking his thumb, stroking the bear's coat, feeling the firelight upon his face, he felt that now something would occur. He had realised that there was much to explore and that, after all, perhaps there might be more in this strange condition of things than he had only a little time ago considered possible. It was then that he looked up and saw hanging round his mother's neck a gold chain. This was a long chain hanging right down to her lap; as it hung there, very slowly it swayed from side to side, and as it swayed, the firelight caught it and it gleamed and was splashed with light. His eyes, as he watched, grew rounder and rounder; he had never seen anything so wonderful. He put down the rattle, crawled, with great difficulty because of his long clothes, on to his knees and sat staring, his thumb in his mouth. His mother stayed, watching him. He pointed his finger, crowing. "Come and fetch it," she said.

He tumbled forward on to his nose and then lay there, with his face raised a little, watching it. She did not move at all, but knelt with her hands straight out upon her knees, and the chain with its large gold rings like flaming eyes swung from hand to hand. Then he tried to move forward, his whole soul in his gaze. He would raise a hand towards the treasure and then because that upset his balance he would fall, but at once he would be up again. He moved a little and breathed little gasps of pleasure.

She bent forward to him, his hand was outstretched. His eyes went up and, meeting hers, instantly the chain was forgotten. That recognition that they had given him before was there now.

With a scramble and a lurch, desperate, heedless in its risks, he was in his mother's lap. Then he crowed. He crowed for all the world to hear because now, at last, he had become its citizen.

Was there not then, from some one, disregarded and forgotten at that moment, a sigh, lighter than the air itself, half-ironic, half-wistful regret?

Hugh Walpole

CHAPTER II

ERNEST HENRY

I

Young Ernest Henry Wilberforce, who had only yesterday achieved his second birthday, watched, with a speculative eye, his nurse. He was seated on the floor with his back to the high window that was flaming now with the light of the dying sun; his nurse was by the fire, her head, shadowed huge and fantastic on the wall, nodded and nodded and nodded. Ernest Henry was, in figure, stocky and square, with a head round, hard, and covered with yellow curls; rather light and cold blue eyes and a chin of no mean degree were further possessions. He was wearing a white blouse, a white skirt, white socks and shoes; his legs were fat and bulged above his socks; his cold blue eyes never moved from his nurse's broad back.

He knew that, in a very short time, disturbance would begin. He knew that doors would open and shut, that there would be movement, strange noises, then an attack upon himself, ultimately a removal of him to another place, a stripping off him of his blouse, his skirt, his socks and his shoes, a loathsome and strangely useless application of soap and water—it was only, of course, in later years that he learned the names of those abominable articles—and, finally, finally darkness. All this he felt hovering very close at hand; one nod too many of his nurse's head, and up she would start, off she would go, off *he* would go.... He watched her and stroked very softly his warm, fat calf.

It was a fine, spacious room that he inhabited. The ceiling—very, very far away—was white and glimmering with shadowy spaces of gold flung by the sun across the breast of it. The wallpaper was dark-red, and there were many coloured pictures of ships and dogs and snowy Christmases, and swans eating from the hands of beautiful little girls, and one garden with roses and peacocks and a tumbling fountain. To Ernest Henry these were simply splashes of colour, and colour, moreover, scarcely so convincing as the bright blue screen by the fire, or the golden brown rug by the door; but he was dimly aware that, as the days passed, so did he find more and more to consider in the shapes and sizes between the deep black frames.... There might, after all, be something in it.

But it was not the pictures that he was now considering.

Before his nurse's descent upon him he was determined that he would walk—not crawl, but walk in his socks and shoes—from his place by the window to the blue screen by the fire. There had been days, and those not so long ago, when so hazardous an Odyssey had seemed the vainest of Blue Moon ambitions; it had once been the only rule of existence to sprawl and roll and sprawl again; but gradually some further force had stirred his limbs. It was a finer thing to be upright; there was a finer view, a more lordly sense of possession could be summoned to one's command. That, then, once decided, upright one must be and upright, with many sudden and alarming collapses, Ernest Henry was.

He had marked out, from the first, the distance from the wall to the blue screen as a very decent distance. There was, half-way, a large rocking-chair that would be either a danger or a deliverance, as Fate should have it. Save for this, it was, right across the brown, rose-strewn carpet, naked country. Truly a perilous business. As he sat there and looked at it, his heart a little misgave him; in this strange, new world into which he had been so roughly hustled, amongst a horde of alarming and painful occurrences, he had discovered nothing so disconcerting as that sudden giving of the knees, that rising of the floor to meet you, the collapse, the pain, and above all the disgrace. Moreover, let him fail now, and it meant, in short,—banishment—banishment and then darkness. There were risks. It was the most perilous thing that, in this new country, he had yet attempted, but attempt it he would.... He was as obstinate as his chin could make him.

With his blue eyes still cautiously upon his nurse's shadow he raised himself very softly, his fat hand pressed against the wall, his mouth tightly closed, and from between his teeth there issued the most distant relation of that sound that the traditional ostler makes when he is cleaning down a horse. His knees quivered, straightened; he was up. Far away in the long, long distance were piled the toys that yesterday's birthday had given him. They did not, as yet, mean anything to him at all. One day, perhaps when he had torn the dolls limb from limb, twisted the railways until they stood end upon end in sheer horror, disembowelled the bears and golliwogs so that they screamed again, he might have some personal feeling for them. At present there they lay in shining impersonal newness, and there for Ernest Henry they might lie for ever.

For an instant, his hand against the wall, he was straight and motionless; then he took his hand away, and his journey began. At the first movement a strange, an amazing glory filled him. From the instant, two years ago, of his first arrival he had been disturbed by an irritating sense of inadequacy; he had been sent, it seemed, into this new and tiresome condition of things without any fitting provisions for his real needs. Demands were always made upon him that were, in the absurd lack of ways and means, impossible of fulfilment. But now, at last, he was using the world as it should be used.... He was fine, he was free, he was absolutely master. His legs might shake, his body lurch from side to side, his breath come in agitating gasps and whistles; the wall was now far behind him, the screen most wonderfully near, the rocking-chair almost within his grasp. Great and mighty is Ernest Henry

Wilberforce, dazzling and again dazzling the lighted avenues opening now before him; there is nothing, nothing, from the rendings of the toys to the deliberate defiance of his nurse and all those in authority over him, that he shall not now perform.... With a cry, with a wild wave of the arms, with a sickening foretaste of the bump with which the gay brown carpet would mark him, he was down, the Fates were upon him—the disturbance, the disrobing, the darkness. Nevertheless, even as he was carried, sobbing, into the farther room, there went with him a consciousness that life would never again be quite the dull, purposeless, monotonous thing that it had hitherto been.

II

After a long time he was alone. About him the room, save for the yellow night-light above his head, was dark, humped with shadows, with grey pools of light near the windows, and a golden bar that some lamp beyond the house flung upon the wall. Ernest Henry lay and, now and again, cautiously felt the bump on his forehead; there was butter on the bump, and an interesting confusion and pain and importance round and about it. Ernest Henry's eyes sought the golden bar, and then, lingering there, looked back upon the recent adventure. He had walked; yes, he had walked. This would, indeed, be something to tell his Friend.

His friend, he knew, would be very shortly with him. It was not every night that he came, but always, before his coming, Ernest Henry knew of his approach—knew by the happy sense of comfort that stole softly about him, knew by the dismissal of all those fears and shapes and terrors that, otherwise, so easily beset him. He sucked his thumb now, and felt his bump, and stared at the ceiling and knew that he would come. During the first months after Ernest Henry's arrival on this planet his friend was never absent from him at all, was always there, drawing through his fingers the threads of the old happy life and the new alarming one, mingling them so that the

Hugh Walpole

transition from the one to the other might not be too sharp—
reassuring, comforting, consoling. Then there had been hours
when he had withdrawn himself, and that earlier world had
grown a little vaguer, a little more remote, and certain things,
certain foods and smells and sounds had taken their place
within the circle of realised facts. Then it had come to be that
the friend only came at night, came at that moment when the
nurse had gone, when the room was dark, and the possible
beasts—the first beast, the second beast, and the third beast—
began to creep amongst those cool, grey shadows in the hollow
of the room. He always came then, was there with his arm
about Ernest Henry, his great body, his dark beard, his large,
firm hands—all so reassuring that the beasts might do the
worst, and nothing could come of it. He brought with him,
indeed, so much more than himself—brought a whole world
of recollected wonders, of all that other time when Ernest
Henry had other things to do, other disciplines, other
triumphs, other defeats, and other glories. Of late his memory
of the other time had been untrustworthy. Things during the
day-time would remind him, but would remind him,
nevertheless, with a strange mingling of the world at present
about him, so that he was not sure of his visions. But when his
friend was with him the memories were real enough, and it was
the nurse, the fire, the red wallpaper, the smell of toast, the
taste of warm milk, that were faint and shadowy.

His friend was there, just as always, suddenly sitting there on
the bed with his arm round Ernest Henry's body, his dark
beard just tickling Ernest Henry's neck, his hand tight about
Ernest Henry's hand. They told one another things in the old
way without tiresome words and sounds; but, for the benefit of
those who are unfortunately too aged to remember that old
and pleasant intercourse, one must make use of the English
language. Ernest Henry displayed his bump, and explained its
origin; and then, even as he did so, was aware that the reality
of the bump made the other world just a little less real. He was
proud that he had walked and stood up, and had been the
master of his circumstance; but just because he had done so he
was aware that his friend was a little, a very little farther away

to-night than he had ever been before.

"Well, I'm very glad that you're going to stand on your own, because you'll have to. I'm going to leave you now—leave you for longer, far longer than I've ever left you before."

"Leave me?"

"Yes. I shan't always be with you; indeed, later on you won't want me. Then you'll forget me, and at last you won't even believe that I ever existed—until, at the end of it all, I come to take you away. *Then* it will all come back to you."

"Oh, but that's absurd!" Ernest Henry said confidently. Nevertheless, in his heart he knew that, during the day-time, other things did more and more compel his attention. There were long stretches during the day-time now when he forgot his friend.

"After your second birthday I always leave you more to yourselves. I shall go now for quite a time, and you'll see that when the old feeling comes, and you know that I'm coming back, you'll be quite startled and surprised that you'd got on so well without me. Of course, some of you want me more than others do, and with some of you I stay quite late in life. There are one or two I never leave at all. But you're not like that; you'll get on quite well without me."

"Oh, no, I shan't," said Ernest Henry, and he clung very tightly and was most affectionate. But he suddenly put his fingers to his bump, felt the butter, and his chin shot up with self-satisfaction.

"To-morrow I'll get ever so much farther," he said.

"You'll behave, and not mind the beasts or the creatures?" his friend said. "You must remember that it's not the slightest use to call for me. You're on your own. Think of me, though. Don't forget me altogether. And don't forget all the other

Hugh Walpole

world in your new discoveries. Look out of the window sometimes. That will remind you more than anything."

He had kissed him, had put his hand for a moment on Ernest Henry's curls, and was gone. Ernest Henry, his thumb in his mouth, was fast asleep.

III

Suddenly, with a wild, agonising clutch at the heart, he was awake. He was up in bed, his hands, clammy and hot, pressed together, his eyes staring, his mouth dry. The yellow night-light was there, the bars of gold upon the walls, the cool, grey shadows, the white square of the window; but there, surely, also, were the beasts. He knew that they were there—one crouching right away there in the shadow, all black, damp; one crawling, blacker and damper, across the floor; one—yes, beyond question—one, the blackest and cruellest of them all, there beneath the bed. The bed seemed to heave, the room flamed with terror. He thought of his friend; on other nights he had invoked him, and instantly there had been assurance and comfort. Now that was of no avail; his friend would not come. He was utterly alone. Panic drove him; he thought that there, on the farther side of the bed, claws and a black arm appeared. He screamed and screamed and screamed.

The door was flung open, there were lights, his nurse appeared. He was lying down now, his face towards the wall, and only dry, hard little sobs came from him. Her large red hand was upon his shoulder, but brought no comfort with it. Of what use was she against the three beasts? A poor creature.... He was ashamed that he should cry before her. He bit his lip.

"Dreaming, I suppose, sir," she said to some one behind her. Another figure came forward. Some one sat down on the edge of the bed, put his arm round Ernest Henry's body and drew him towards him. For one wild moment Ernest Henry fancied that his friend had, after all, returned. But no. He knew that these were the conditions of this world, not of that other. When he crept close to his friend he was caught up into a soft, rosy comfort, was conscious of nothing except ease and rest. Here there were knobs and hard little buttons, and at first his head was pressed against a cold, slippery surface that hurt. Nevertheless, the pressure was pleasant and comforting. A warm hand stroked his hair. He liked it, jerked his head up, and hit his new friend's chin.

"Oh, damn!" he heard quite clearly. This was a new sound to Ernest Henry; but just now he was interested in sounds, and had learnt lately quite a number. This was a soft, pleasant, easy sound. He liked it.

And so, with it echoing in his head, his curly head against his father's shoulder, the bump glistening in the candle-light, the beasts defeated and derided, he tumbled into sleep.

IV

A pleasant sight at breakfast was Ernest Henry, with his yellow curls gleaming from his bath, his bib tied firmly under his determined chin, his fat fingers clutching a large spoon, his body barricaded into a high chair, his heels swinging and kicking and swinging again. Very fine, too, was the nursery on a sunny morning—the fire crackling, the roses on the brown carpet as lively as though they were real, and the whole place glittering, glowing with size and cleanliness and vigour. In the air was the crackling smell of toast and bacon, in a glass dish was strawberry jam, through the half-open window came all the fun of the Square—the sparrows, the carts, the motor-cars, the bells, and horses.... Oh, a fine morning was fine indeed!

Ernest Henry, deep in the business of conveying securely his bread and milk from the bowl—a beautiful bowl with red robins all round the outside of it—to his mouth, laughed at the three beasts. Let them show themselves here in the sunlight, and they'd see what they'd get. Let them only dare!

He surveyed, with pleased anticipation, the probable progress of his day. He glanced at the pile of toys in the farther corner of the room, and thought to himself that he might, after all, find some diversion there. Yesterday they had seemed disappointing; to-day in the glow of the sun they suggested, adventure. Then he looked towards that stretch of country—that wall-to-screen marathon—and, with an eye upon his nurse, meditated a further attempt. He put down his spoon, and felt his bump. It was better; perchance there would be two bumps by the evening. And then, suddenly, he remembered.... He felt again the terror, saw the lights and his nurse, then that new friend.... He pondered, lifted his spoon, waved it in the air; and then smiling with the happy recovery of a pleasant, friendly sound, repeated half to himself, half to his nurse: "Damn! Damn! Damn!"

That began for him the difficulties of his day. He was hustled, shaken; words, words, words were poured down upon him. He understood that, in some strange, unexpected, bewildering fashion he had done wrong. There was nothing more puzzling in his present surroundings than that amazingly sudden transition from serenity to danger. Here one was, warm with food, bathed in sunlight, with a fine, ripe day in front of one.... Then the mere murmur of a sound, and all was tragedy.

He hated his toys, his nurse, his food, his world; he sat in a corner of the room and glowered.... How was he to know? If, under direct encouragement, he could be induced to say "dada," or "horse," or "twain," he received nothing but applause and, often enough, reward. Yet, let him make use of that pleasant new sound that he had learnt, and he was in disgrace. Upon this day, more than any other in his young life, he ached, he longed for some explanation. Then, sitting there in his corner, there came to him a discovery, the force of which was never, throughout all his later life, to leave him. He had been deserted by his friend. His last link with that other life was broken. He was here, planted in the strangest of strange places, with nothing whatever to help him. He was alone; he must fight for his own hand. He would—from that moment, seated there beneath the window, Ernest Henry Wilberforce challenged the terrors of this world, and found them sawdust—he would say "damn" as often as he pleased. "Damn, damn, damn, damn," he whispered, and marked again, with meditative eye, the space from wall to screen.

After this, greatly cheered, he bethought him of the Square. Last night his friend had said to him that when he wished to think of him, and go back for a time to the other world, a peep into the Square would assist him. He clambered up on to the window-seat, caught behind him those sounds, "Now, Master Ernest," which he now definitely connected with condemnation and disapproval, shook his curls in defiance, and pressed his nose to the glass. The Square was a dazzling sight. He had not as yet names for any of the things that he saw there, nor, when he went out on his magnificent daily progress in his perambulator did he associate the things that he found immediately around him with the things that he saw from his lofty window; but, with every absorbed gaze they stood more securely before him, and were fixed ever more firmly in his memory.

This was a Square with fine, white, lofty houses, and in the houses were an infinite number of windows, sometimes gay and sometimes glittering. In the middle of the Square was a garden, and in the middle of the garden, very clearly visible from Ernest Henry's window, was a fountain. It was this fountain, always tossing and leaping, that gave Ernest Henry the key to his memories. Gazing at it he had no difficulty at all to find himself back in the old life. Even now, although only two years had passed, it was difficult not to reveal his old experiences by means of terms of his new discoveries. He thought, for instance, of the fountain as a door that led into the country whose citizen he had once been, and that country he saw now in terms of doors and passages and rooms and windows, whereas, in reality, it had been quite otherwise.

Hugh Walpole

But now, perched up there on the window-sill, he felt that if he could only bring the fountain in with him out of the Square into his nursery, he would have the key to both existences. He wanted to understand—to understand what was the relation between his friend who had left last night, why he might say "dada," but mustn't say "damn," why, finally, he was here at all. He did not consciously consider these things; his brain was only very slightly, as yet, concerned in his discoveries; but, like a flowing river, beneath his movements and actions, the interplay of his two existences drove him on through, his adventure.

There were, of course, many other things in the Square besides the fountain. There was, at the farther corner, just out of the Square, but quite visible from Ernest Henry's window, a fruit-shop with coloured fruit piled high on the boards outside the windows. Indeed, that side street, of which one could only catch this glimpse, promised to be most wonderful always; when evening came a golden haze hovered round and about it. In the garden itself there were often many children, and for an hour every afternoon Ernest Henry might be found amongst them. There were two statues in the Square—one of a gentleman in a beard and a frock-coat, the other of a soldier riding very finely upon a restless horse; but Ernest Henry was not, as yet, old enough to realise the meaning and importance of these heroes.

Outside the Square there were many dogs, and even now as he looked down from his window he could see a number of them, black and brown and white.

The trees trembled in a little breeze, the fountain flashed in the sun, somewhere a barrel-organ was playing.... Ernest Henry gave a little sigh, of satisfaction.

He was back! He was back! He was slipping, slipping into distance through the window into the street, under the fountain, its glittering arms had caught him; he was up, the door was before him, he had the key.

"Time for you to put your things on, Master Ernest. And 'ow you've dirtied your knees! There! Look!"

He shook himself, clambered down from the window, gave his nurse what she described as "One of his old, old looks. Might be eighty when he's like that.... They're all like it when they're young."

With a sigh he translated himself back into this new, tiresome existence.

V

But after that morning things were never again quite the same. He gave himself up deliberately to the new life.

With that serious devotion towards anything likely to be of real practical value to him that was, in his later years, never to fail him, he attacked this business of "words." He discovered that if he made certain sounds when certain things were said to him he provoked instant applause. He liked popularity; he liked the rewards that popularity brought him. He acquired a formula that amounted practically to "Wash dat?" And whenever he saw anything new he produced his question. He learnt with amazing rapidity. He was, his nurse repeatedly told his father, "a most remarkable child."

It could not truthfully be said that during these weeks he forgot his friend altogether. There were still the dark hours at night when he longed for him, and once or twice he had cried aloud for him. But slowly that slipped away. He did not look often now at the fountain.

There were times when his friend was almost there. One evening, kneeling on the floor before the fire, arranging shining soldiers in a row, he was aware of something that made him sharply pause and raise his head. He was, for the moment, alone in the room that was glowing and quivering now in the firelight. The faint stir and crackle of the fire, the rich flaming colour that rose and fell against the white ceiling might have been enough to make him wonder. But there was also the scent of a clump of blue hyacinths standing in shadow by the darkened window, and this scent caught him, even as the fountain had caught him, caught him with the stillness, the leaping fire, the twisted sense of romantic splendours that came, like some magician's smoke and flame, up to his very heart and brain. He did not turn his head, but behind him he was sure, there on the golden-brown rug, his friend was standing, watching him with his smiling eyes, his dark beard; he would be ready, at the least movement, to catch him up and hold him. Swiftly, Ernest Henry turned. There was no one there.

But those moments were few now; real people were intervening. He had no mother, and this was doubtless the reason why his nurse darkly addressed him as "Poor Lamb" on many occasions; but he was, of course, at present unaware of his misfortune. He *had* an aunt, and of this lady he was aware only too vividly. She was long and thin and black, and he would not have disliked her so cordially, perhaps, had he not from the very first been aware of the sharpness of her nose when she kissed him. Her nose hurt him, and so he hated her. But, as he grew, he discovered that this hatred was well-founded. Miss Wilberforce had not a happy way with children; she was nervous when she should have been bold, and secret when she should have been honesty itself. When Ernest Henry was the merest atom in a cradle, he discovered that she was afraid of him; he hated the shiny stuff of her dress. She wore a gold chain that—when you pulled it—snapped and hit your fingers. There were sharp pins at the back of her dress. He hated her; he was not afraid of her, and yet on that critical night when his friend told him of his departure, it was the fear of being left alone with the black cold shiny thing that troubled him most; she bore of all the daylight things the closest resemblance to the three beasts.

There was, of course, his nurse, and a great deal of his time was spent in her company; but she had strangely little connection with his main problem of the relation of this, his present world, to that, his preceding one. She was there to answer questions, to issue commands, to forbid. She had the key to various cupboards—to the cupboard with pretty cups and jam and sugar, to the cupboard with ugly things that tasted horrible, things that he resisted by instinct long before they arrived under his nose. She also had certain sounds, of which she made invariable use on all occasions. One was, "Now, Master Ernest!" Another: "Mind-what-you're-about-now!" And, at his "Wash dat!" always "Oh-bother-the-boy!" She was large and square to look upon, very often pins were in her mouth, and the slippers that she wore within doors often clipclapped upon the carpet. But she was not a person; she had nothing to do with his progress.

The person who had to do with it was, of course, his father. That night when his friend had left him had been, indeed, a crisis, because it was on that night that his father had come to him. It was not that he had not been aware of his father before, but he had been aware of him only as he had been aware of light and heat and food. Now it had become a definite wonder as to whether this new friend had been sent to take the place of the old one. Certainly the new friend had very little to do with all that old life of which the fountain was the door. He belonged, most definitely, to the new one, and everything about him—the delightfully mysterious tick of his gold watch, the solid, firm grasp of his hand, the sure security of his shoulder upon which Ernest Henry now gloriously rode— these things were of this world and none other.

It was a different relationship, this, from any other that Ernest Henry had ever known, but there was no doubt at all about its pleasant flavour. Just as in other days he had watched for his friend's appearance, so now he waited for that evening hour that always brought his father. The door would open, the square, set figure would appear.... Very pleasant, indeed. Meanwhile Ernest Henry was instructed that the right thing to say on his father's appearance was "Dada."

But he knew better. His father's name was really "Damn."

VI

The days and weeks passed. There had been no sign of his friend.... Then the crisis came.

That old wall-to-screen marathon had been achieved, and so contemptuously banished. There was now the great business of marching without aid from one end of the room to the other. This was a long business, and always hitherto somewhere about the middle of it Ernest Henry had sat down suddenly, pretending, even to himself, that his shoe *hurt*, or that he was bored with the game, and would prefer some other.

There came, then, a beautiful spring evening. The long low evening sun flooded the room, and somewhere a bell was calling Christian people to their prayers, and somewhere else the old man with the harp, who always came round the Square once every week, was making beautiful music.

Ernest Henry's father had taken the nurse's place for an hour, and was reading a *Globe* with absorbed attention by the window; Mr. Wilberforce, senior, was one of London's most famous barristers, and the *Globe* on this particular afternoon had a great deal to say about this able man's cleverness. Ernest Henry watched his father, watched the light, heard the bell and the harp, felt that the hour was ripe for his attempt.

He started, and, even as he did so, was aware that, after he had succeeded in this great adventure, things—that is, life—would never be quite the same again. He knew by now every stage of the first half of his journey. The first instalment was defined by that picture of the garden and the roses and the peacocks; the second by the beginning of the square brown nursery table; and here there was always a swift and very testing temptation to cling, with a sticky hand, to the hard and shining corner. The third division was the end of the nursery table where one was again tempted to give the corner a final clutch before passing forth into the void. After this there was nothing, no rest, no possible harbour until the end.

Off Ernest Henry started. He could see his father, there in the long distance, busied with his paper; he could see the nursery table, with bright-blue and red reels of cotton that nurse had left there; he could see a discarded railway engine that lay gaping there half-way across, ready to catch and trip him if he were not careful. His eyes were like saucers, the hissing noise came from between his teeth, his forehead frowned. He passed the peacock, he flung contemptuously aside the proffered corner of the table; he passed, as an Atlantic liner passes the Eddystone, the table's other end; he was on the last stretch.

Then suddenly he paused. He lifted his head, caught with his eye a pink, round cloud that sailed against the evening blue beyond the window, heard the harpist, heard his father turn and exclaim, as he saw him.

He knew, as he stood there, that at last the moment had come. His friend had returned.

All the room was buzzing with it. The dolls fell in a neglected heap, the train on the carpet, the fire behind the fender, the reels of cotton that were on the table—they all knew it.

His friend had returned.

His impulse was, there and then, to sit down.

His friend was whispering: "Come along!... Come along!... Come along!" He knew that, on his surrender, his father would make sounds like, "Well, old man, tired, eh? Bed, I suggest." He knew that bed would follow. Then darkness, then his friend.

For an instant there was fierce battle between the old forces and the new. Then, with his eyes upon his father, resuming

Hugh Walpole

that hiss that is proper only to ostlers, he continued his march.

He reached the wall. He caught his father's leg. He was raised on to his father's lap, was kissed, was for a moment triumphant; then suddenly burst into tears.

"Why, old man, what's the matter?"

But Ernest Henry could not explain. Had he but known it he had, in that rejection of his friend, completed the first stage of his "Pilgrimage from this world to the next."

CHAPTER III

ANGELINA

I

Angelina Braid, on the morning of her third birthday, woke very early. It would be too much to say that she knew it was her birthday, but she awoke, excited. She looked at the glimmering room, heard the sparrows beyond her windows, heard the snoring of her nurse in the large bed opposite her own, and lay very still, with her heart thumping like anything. She made no noise, however, because it was not her way to make a noise. Angelina Braid was the quietest little girl in all the Square. "You'd never meet one nigher a mouse in a week of Sundays," said her nurse, who was a "gay one" and liked life.

It was not, however, entirely Angelina's fault that she took life quietly; in 21 March Square, it was exceedingly difficult to do anything else. Angelina's parents were in India, and she was not conscious, very acutely, of their existence. Every morning and evening she prayed, "God bless mother and father in India," but then she was not very acutely conscious of God either, and so her mind was apt to wander during her prayers.

She lived with her two aunts—Miss Emmy Braid and Miss Violet Braid—in the smallest house in the Square. So slim was No. 21, and so ruthlessly squeezed between the opulent No. 20 and the stout ruddy-faced No. 22, that it made one quite

Hugh Walpole

breathless to look at it; it was exactly as though an old maid, driven by suffragette wildness, had been arrested by two of the finest possible policemen, and carried off into custody. Very little of any kind of wildness was there about the Misses Braid. They were slim, neat women, whose rather yellow faces had the flat, squashed look of lawn grass after a garden roller has passed over it. They believed in God according to the Reverend Stephen Hunt, of St. Matthew-in-the-Crescent—the church round the corner—but in no other kind of God whatever. They were not rich, and they were not poor; they went once a week—Fridays—to visit the poor of St. Matthew's, and found the poor of St. Matthew's on the whole unappreciative of their efforts, but that made their task the nobler. Their house was dark and musty, and filled with little articles left them by their grand-parents, their parents, and other defunct relations. They had no friendly feeling towards one another, but missed one another when they were separated. They were, both of them, as strong as horses, but very hypochondriacal, and Dr. Armstrong of Mulberry Place made a very pleasant little income out of them.

I have mentioned them at length, because they had a great deal to do with Angelina's quiet behaviour. No. 21 was not a house that welcomed a child's ringing laughter. But, in any case, the Misses Braid were not fond of children, but only took Angelina because they had a soft spot in their dry hearts for their brother Jim, and in any case it would have been difficult to say no.

Their attitude to children was that they could not understand why they did not instantly see things as they, their elders, saw them; but then, on the other hand, if an especially bright child did take a grown-up point of view about anything *that* was considered "forward" and "conceited," so that it was really very difficult for Angelina.

"It's a pity Jim's got such a dull child," Miss Violet would say. "You never would have expected it."

"What I like about a child," said Miss Emmy, "is a little cheerfulness and natural spirit—not all this moping."

Angelina was not, on the whole, popular.... The aunts had very little idea of making a house cheerful for a child. The room allotted to Angelina as a nursery was at the top of the house, and had once been a servant's bedroom. It possessed two rather grimy windows, a faded brown wallpaper, an old green carpet, and some very stiff, hard chairs. On one wall was a large map of the world, and on the other an old print of Romans sacking Jerusalem, a picture which frightened Angelina every night of her life, when the dark came and the lamp illuminated the writhing limbs, the falling bodies, the tottering walls. From the windows the Square was visible, and at the windows Angelina spent a great deal of her time, but her present nurse—nurses succeeded one another with startling frequency—objected to what she called "window-gazing." "Makes a child dreamy," she said; "lowers her spirits."

Angelina was, naturally, a dreamy child, and no amount of nurses could prevent her being one. She was dreamy because her loneliness forced her to be so, and if her dreams were the most real part of her day to her that was surely the faults of her aunts. But she was not at all a quick child; although to-day was her third birthday she could not talk very well, could not pronounce her r's, and lisped in what her trail of nurses told her was a ridiculous fashion for so big a girl. But, then, she was not really a big girl; her figure was short and stumpy, her features plain and pale with the pallor of her first Indian year. Her eyes were large and black and rather fine.

On this morning she lay in bed, and knew that she was excited because her friend had come the night before and told her that to-day would be an important day. Angelina clung, with a desperate tenacity, to her memories of everything that happened to her before her arrival on this unpleasant planet. Those memories now were growing faint, and they came to her only in flashes, in sudden twists and turns of the scene, as though she were surrounded by curtains and, every now and then, was allowed a peep through. Her friend had been with her continually at first, and, whilst he had been there, the old life had been real and visible enough; but on her second birthday he had told her that it was right now that she should manage by herself. Since then, he had come when she least expected him; sometimes when she had needed him very badly he had not appeared.... She never knew. At any rate, he had said that to-day would be important.... She lay in bed, listening to her nurse's snores, and waited.

II

At breakfast she knew that it was her birthday. There were presents from her aunts—a picture-book and a box of pencils—there was also a mysterious parcel. Angelina could not remember that she had ever had a parcel before, and the excitement of this one must be prolonged. She would not open it, but gazed at it, with her spoon in the air and her mouth wide open.

"Come, Miss Angelina—what a name to give the poor lamb!—get on with your breakfast now, or you'll never have done. Why not open the pretty parcel?"

"No. Do you think it is a twain?"

"Say train—not twain."

"Train."

"No, of course not; not a thing that shape."

"Oh! Do you think it's a bear?"

"Maybe—maybe. Come now, get on with your bread and butter."

"Don't want any more."

"Get down from your chair, then. Say your grace now."

"Thank God nice bweakfast, Amen."

"That's right! Now open it, then."

"No, not now."

"Drat the child! Well, wipe your face, then."

Angelina carried her parcel to the window, and then, after gazing at it for a long time, at last opened it. Her eyes grew wider and wider, her chubby fingers trembled. Nurse undid the wrappings of paper, slowly folded up the sheets, then produced, all naked and unashamed, a large rag doll.

"There! There's a pretty thing for you, Miss 'Lina."

She had her hand about the doll's head, and held her there, suspended.

"Give her me! Give her me!" Angelina rescued her, and, with eyes flaming, the doll laid lengthways in her arms, tottered off to the other corner of the room.

"Well, there's gratitude," said the nurse, "and never asking so much as who it's from."

But nurse, aunts, all the troubles and disappointments of this world had vanished from Angelina's heart and soul. She had seen, at that first glimpse that her nurse had so rudely given her, that here at last, after long, long waiting, was the blessing that she had so desired. She had had other dolls—quite a number of them. Even now Lizzie (without an eye) and Rachel (rather fine in bridesmaid's attire) were leaning their disconsolate backs against the boarding beneath the window seat. There had been, besides Rachel and Lizzie, two Annies, a Mary, a May, a Blackamoor, a Jap, a Sailor, and a Baby in a Bath. They were now as though they had never been; Angelina knew with absolute certainty of soul, with that blending of will and desire, passion, self-sacrifice and absence of humour that must inevitably accompany true love that here was her Fate.

"It's been sent you by your kind Uncle Teny," said nurse. "You'll have to write a nice letter and thank him."

*   *   *   *   *

But Angelina knew better. She—a name had not yet been chosen—had been sent to her by her friend.... He had promised her last night that this should be a day of days.

Her aunts, appearing to receive thanks where thanks were due, darkened the doorway.

"Good-morning, mum. Good-morning, mum. Now, Miss 'Lina, thank your kind aunties for their beautiful presents."

She stood up, clutching the doll.

"T'ank you, Auntie Vi'let; t'ank you, Auntie Em'ly—your lovely pwesents."

"That's right, Angelina. I hope you'll use them sensibly. What's that she's holding, nurse?"

"It's a doll Mr. Edward's sent her, mum."

"What a hideous creature! Edward might have chosen something—Time for her to go out, nurse, I think—now, while the sun's warm."

But she did not hear. She did not know that they had gone. She sat there in a dreamy ecstasy rocking the red-cheeked creature in her arms, seeing, with her black eyes, visions and the beauty of a thousand worlds.

III

The name Rose was given to her. Rose had been kept, as a name, until some one worthy should arrive.... "Wosie Bwaid," a very good name. Her nakedness was clothed first in Rachel's bridesmaid's attire—alas! Poor Rachel!—but the lace and finery did not suit those flaming red cheeks and beady black eyes. Rose was, there could be no question, a daughter of the soil; good red blood ran through her stout veins. Tess of the countryside, your laughing, chaffing, arms-akimbo dairymaid; no poor white product of the over-civilised cities. Angelina felt that the satin and lace were wrong; she tore them off, searched in the heaped-up cupboard for poor neglected Annie No. 1, found her, tore from her her red woollen skirt and white blouse, stretched them about Rose's portly body.

"T'ank God for nice Wose, Amen," she said, but she meant, not God, but her friend. He, her friend, had never sent her anything before, and now that Rose had come straight from him, she must have a great deal to tell her about him. Nothing puzzled her more than the distressing fact that she wondered sometimes whether her friend was ever really coming again, whether any of the wonderful things that were happening on every side of her wouldn't suddenly one fine morning vanish altogether, and leave her to a dreary world of nurse, bread and milk, and the Romans sacking Jerusalem. She didn't, of course, put it like that; all that it meant to her was that stupid people and tiresome things were always interfering between herself and *real* fun. Now it was time to go out, now to go to bed, now to eat, now to be taken downstairs into that horrid room where she couldn't move because things would tumble off the tables so ... all this prevented her own life when she would sit and try, and try, and remember *what* it was all like once, and wonder why when once things had been so beautiful they were so ugly and disappointing now.

Now Rose had come, and she could talk to Rose about it. "What she sees in that ugly old doll!" said the nurse to the housemaid. "You can take my word, Mary, she'll sit in that window looking down at the gardens, nursing that rag and just say nothing. It fair gives you the creeps ... left too much to herself, the poor child is. As for those old women downstairs, if I 'ad my way—but there! Living's living, and bread and butter's bread and butter!"

But, of course, Angelina's heart was bursting with affection, and there had been, until Rose's arrival, no one upon whom she might bestow it. Rose might seem to the ordinary observer somewhat unresponsive. She sat there, whether it were tea-time, dressing-time, bed-time, always staring in front of her, her mouth closed, her arms, bow-shaped, standing stiffly away from her side, taking, it might seem, but little interest in her mistress's confidences. Did one give her tea she only dribbled at the lip; did one place upon her head a straw hat with red ribbon torn from poor May—once a reigning favourite—she made no effort to keep it upon her head. Jewels and gold could rouse no appreciation from her; she was sunk in a lethargy that her rose-red cheeks most shamefully belied.

But Angelina had the key to her. Angelina understood that confiding silence, appreciated that tactful discretion, adored that complete submission to her will. It was true that her friend had only come once to her now within the space of many, many weeks, but he had sent her Rose. "He's coming soon, Wose—weally soon—to tell us stowies. Bu-ootiful ones."

She sat, gazing down into the Square, and her dreams were longer and longer and longer.

IV

Miss Emily Braid was a softer creature than her sister, and she had, somewhere in her heart, some sort of affection for her niece. She made, now and then, little buccaneering raids upon the nursery, with the intention of arriving at some intimate terms with that strange animal. But she had no gift of ease with children; her attempts at friendliness were viewed by Angelina with the gravest suspicion and won no return. This annoyed Miss Emily, and because she was conscious that she herself was in reality to blame, she attacked Angelina all the more fiercely. "This brooding must be stopped," she said. "Really, it's most unhealthy."

It was quite impossible for her to believe that a child of three could really be interested by golden sunsets, the colours of the fountain that was in the centre of the gardens, the soft, grey haze that clothed the houses on a spring evening; and when, therefore, she saw Angelina gazing at these things, she decided that the child was morbid. Any interest, however, that Angelina may have taken in her aunts before Rose's arrival was now reduced to less than nothing at all.

"That doll that Edward gave the child," said Miss Emily to her sister, "is having a very bad effect on her. Makes her more moody than ever."

"Such a hideous thing!" said Miss Violet. "Well, I shall take it away if I see much more of this nonsense."

It was lucky for Rose meanwhile that she was of a healthy constitution. The meals, the dressing and undressing, the perpetual demands upon her undivided attention, the sudden rousings from her sleep, the swift rockings back into slumber again, the appeals for response, the abuses for indifference, these things would have slain within a week one of her more feeble sisters. But Rose was made of stern stuff, and her rosy cheeks were as rosy, the brightness of her eyes was undimmed. We may believe—and surely many harder demands are made upon our faith—that there did arise a very special relationship between these two. The whole of Angelina's heart was now devoted to Rose's service, Rose's was not devoted to Angelina?... And always Angelina wondered when her friend would return, watched for him in the dusk, awoke in the early mornings and listened for him, searched the Square with its trees and its fountain for his presence.

"Wosie, when did he say he'd come next?" But Rose could not tell. There *were* times when Rose's impenetrability was, to put it at its mildest, aggravating.

Meanwhile, the situation with Aunt Emily grew serious. Angelina was aware that Aunt Emily disliked Rose, and her mouth now shut very tightly and her eyes glared defiance when she thought of this, but her difference with her aunt went more deeply than this. She had known for a long, long time that both her aunts would stop her "dreaming" if they could. Did she tell them about her friend, about the kind of pictures of which the fountain reminded her, about the vivid, lively memories that the tree with the pink flowers—the almond tree—in the corner of the gardens—you could just see it from the nursery window—called to her mind; she knew that she would be punished—put in the corner, or even sent to bed. She did not think these things out consecutively in her mind, but she knew that the dark room downstairs, the dark passages, the stillness and silence of it all frightened her, and that it was always out of these things that her aunts rose.

At night when she lay in bed with Rosie clasped tightly to her, she whispered endlessly about the gardens, the fountain, the barrel organs, the dogs, the other children in the Square—she had names of her own for all these things—and him, who belonged, of course, to the world outside.... Then her whisper would sink, and she would warn Rose about the rooms downstairs, the dining-room with the black chairs, the soft carpet, and the stuffed birds in glass cases—for these things, too, she had names. Here was the hand of death and destruction, the land of crooked stairs, sudden dark doors, mysterious bells and drippings of water—out of all this her aunts came....

Unfortunately it was just at this moment that Miss Emily Braid decided that it was time to take her niece in hand. "The child's three, Violet, and very backward for her age. Why, Mrs. Mancaster's little girl, who's just Angelina's age, can talk fluently, and is beginning with her letters. We don't want Jim to be disappointed in the child when he comes home next year." It would be difficult to determine how much of this was true; Miss Emily was aggravated and, although she would never have confessed to so trivial a matter, the perpetual worship of Rose—"the ugliest thing you ever saw"—was irritating her. The days followed, then, when Angelina was constantly in her aunt's company, and to neither of them was this companionship pleasant.

"You must ask me questions, child. How are you ever going to learn to talk properly if you don't ask me questions?"

"Yes, auntie."

"What's that over there?"

"Twee."

"Say tree, not twee."

"Tree."

"Now look at me. Put that wretched doll down.... Now.... That's right. Now tell me what you've been doing this morning."

"We had bweakfast—nurse said I—(long pause for breath)—was dood girl; Auntie Vi'let came; I dwew with my pencil."

"Say 'drew,' not 'dwew.'"

"Drew."

All this was very exhausting to Aunt Emily. She was no nearer the child's heart.... Angelina maintained an impenetrable reserve. Old maids have much time amongst the unsatisfied and sterile monotonies of their life—this is only true of *some* old maids; there are very delightful ones—to devote to fancies and microscopic imitations. It was astonishing now how largely in Miss Emily Braid's life loomed the figure of Rose, the rag doll.

"If it weren't for that wretched doll, I believe one could get some sense out of the child."

"I think it's a mistake, nurse, to let Miss Angelina play with that doll so much."

"Well, mum, it'd be difficult to take it from her now. She's that wrapped in it." ... And so she was.... Rose stood to Angelina for so much more than Rose.

"Oh, Wosie, *when* will he come again.... P'r'aps never. And I'm forgetting. I can't remember at all about the funny water and the twee with the flowers, and all of it. Wosie, *you* 'member—Whisper." And Rose offered in her own mysterious, taciturn way the desired comfort.

And then, of course, the crisis arrived. I am sorry about this part of the story. Of all the invasions of Aunt Emily, perhaps none were more strongly resented by Angelina than the appropriation of the afternoon hour in the gardens. Nurse had been an admirable escort because, as a lady of voracious appetite for life with, at the moment, but slender opportunities for satisfying it, she was occupied alertly with the possible vision of any male person driven by a similar desire. Her eye wandered; the hand to which Angelina clung was an abstract, imperceptive hand—Angelina and Rose were free to pursue their own train of fancy—the garden was at their service. But with Aunt Emily how different! Aunt Emily pursued relentlessly her educational tactics. Her thin, damp, black glove gripped Angelina's hand; her eyes (they had a "peering" effect, as though they were always searching for something beyond their actual vision) wandered aimlessly about the garden, looking for educational subjects. And so up and down the paths they went, Angelina trotting, with Rose clasped to her breast, walking just a little faster than she conveniently could.

Miss Emily disliked the gardens, and would have greatly preferred that nurse should have been in charge, but this consciousness of trial inflamed her sense of merit. There came a lovely spring afternoon; the almond tree was in full blossom; a cloud of pink against the green hedge, clumps of daffodils rippled with little shudders of delight, even the statues of "Sir Benjamin Bundle" and "General Sir Robinson Cleaver" seemed to unbend a little from their stiff angularity. There were many babies and nurses, and children laughing and crying and shouting, and a sky of mild forget-me-not blue smiled protectingly upon them. Angelina's eyes were fixed upon the fountain, which flashed and sparkled in the air with a happy freedom that seemed to catch all the life of the garden within its heart. Angelina felt how immensely she and Rose might have enjoyed all this had they been alone. Her eyes gazed longingly at the almond tree; she wished that she might go off on a voyage of discovery for, on this day of all days, did its shadow seem to hold some pressing, intimate invitation. "I shall get back—I shall get back.... He'll come and take me; I'll remember all the old things," she thought. She and Rose— what a time they might have if only— She glanced up at her aunt.

"Look at that nice little boy, Angelina," Aunt Emily said. "See how good—" But at that very instant that same playful breeze that had been ruffling the daffodils, and sending shimmers through the fountain decided that now was the moment to catch Miss Emily's black hat at one corner, prove to her that the pin that should have fastened it to her hair was loose, and swing the whole affair to one side. Up went her hands; she gave a little cry of dismay.

Instantly, then, Angelina was determined. She did not suppose that her freedom would be for long, nor did she hope to have time to reach the almond tree; but her small, stumpy legs started off down the path almost before she was aware of it. She started, and Rose bumped against her as she ran. She heard behind her cries; she saw in front of her the almond tree, and then coming swiftly towards her a small boy with a hoop....

Hugh Walpole

She stopped, hesitated, and then fell. The golden afternoon, with all its scents and sounds, passed on above her head. She was conscious that a hand was on her shoulder, she was lifted and shaken. Tears trickling down the side of her nose were checked by little points of gravel. She was aware that the little boy with the hoop had stopped and said something. Above her, very large and grim, was her aunt. Some bird on a tree was making a noise like the drawing of a cork. (She had heard her nurse once draw one.) In her heart was utter misery. The gravel hurt her face, the almond tree was farther away than ever; she was captured more completely than she had ever been before.

"Oh, you naughty little girl—you *naughty* girl," she heard her aunt say; and then, after her, the bird like a cork. She stood there, her mouth tightly shut, the marks of tears drying to muddy lines on her face.

She was dragged off. Aunt Emily was furious at the child's silence; Aunt Emily was also aware that she must have looked what she would call "a pretty figure of fun" with her hat askew, her hair blown "anyway," and a small child of three escaping from her charge as fast as she could go.

Angelina was dragged across the street, in through the squeezed front door, over the dark stairs, up into the nursery. Miss Violet's voice was heard calling, "Is that you, Emily? Tea's been waiting some time."

It was nurse's afternoon out, and the nursery was grimly empty; but through the open, window came the evening sounds of the happy Square. Miss Emily placed Angelina in the middle of the room. "Now say you're sorry, you wicked child!" she exclaimed breathlessly.

"Sowwy," came slowly from Angelina. Then she looked down at her doll.

"Leave that doll alone. Speak as though you were sorry."

"I'm velly sowwy."

"What made you run away like that?" Angelina said nothing. "Come, now! Didn't you know it was very wicked?"

"Yes."

"Well, why did you do it, then?"

"Don't know."

"Don't say 'don't know' like that. You must have had some reason. Don't look at the doll like that. Put the doll down." But this Angelina would not do. She clung to Rose with a ferocious tenacity. I do not think that one must blame Miss Emily for her exasperation. That doll had had a large place in her mind for many weeks. It were as though she, Miss Emily Braid, had been personally, before the world, defied by a rag doll. Her temper, whose control had never been her strongest quality, at the vision of the dirty, obstinate child before her, at the thought of the dancing, mocking gardens behind her, flamed into sudden, trembling rage.

She stepped forward, snatched Rose from Angelina's arms, crossed the room and had pushed the doll, with a fierce, energetic action, as though there was no possible time to be lost, into the fire. She snatched the poker, and with trembling hands pressed the doll down. There was a great flare of flame; Rose lifted one stolid arm to the gods for vengeance, then a stout leg in a last writhing agony. Only then, when it was all concluded, did Aunt Emily hear behind her the little half-strangled cry which made her turn. The child was standing, motionless, with so old, so desperate a gaze of despair that it was something indecent for any human being to watch.

V

Nurse came in from her afternoon. She had heard nothing of

Hugh Walpole

the recent catastrophe, and, as she saw Angelina sitting quietly in front of the fire she thought that she had had her tea, and was now "dreaming" as she so often did. Once, however, as she was busy in another part of the room, she caught half the face in the light of the fire. To any one of a more perceptive nature that glimpse must have seemed one of the most tragic things in the world. But this was a woman of "a sensible, hearty" nature; moreover, her "afternoon" had left her with happy reminiscences of her own charms and their effect on the opposite sex.

She had, however, her moment.... She had left the room to fetch something. Returning she noticed that the dusk had fallen, and was about to switch on the light when, in the rise and fall of the firelight, something that she saw made her pause. She stood motionless by the door.

Angelina had turned in her chair; her eyes were gazing, with rapt attention, toward the purple dusk by the window. She was listening. Nurse, as she had often assured her friends, "was not cursed with imagination," but now fear held her so that she could not stir nor move save that her hand trembled against the wall paper. The chatter of the fire, the shouts of some boys in the Square, the ringing of the bell of St. Matthew's for evensong, all these things came into the room. Angelina, still listening, at last smiled; then, with a little sigh, sat back in her chair.

"Heavens! Miss 'Lina! What were you doing there? How you frightened me!" Angelina left her chair, and went across to the window. "Auntie Emily," she said, "put Wosie into the fire, she did. But Wosie's saved.... He's just come and told me."

"Lord, Miss 'Lina, how you talk!" The room was right again now just as, a moment before, it had been wrong. She switched on the electric light, and, in the sudden blaze, caught the last flicker in the child's eyes of some vision, caught, held, now surrendered.

"'Tis company she's wanting, poor lamb," she thought, "all

this being alone.... Fair gives one the creeps."

She heard with relief the opening of the door. Miss Emily came in, hesitated a moment, then walked over to her niece. In her hands she carried a beautiful doll with flaxen hair, long white robes, and the assured confidence of one who is spotless and knows it.

"There, Angelina," she said. "I oughtn't to have burnt your doll. I'm sorry. Here's a beautiful new one."

Angelina took the spotless one; then with a little thrust of her hand she pushed the half-open window wider apart. Very deliberately she dropped the doll (at whose beauty she had not glanced) out, away, down into the Square.

The doll, white in the dusk, tossed and whirled, and spun finally, a white speck far below, and struck the pavement.

Then Angelina turned, and with a little sigh of satisfaction looked at her aunt.

CHAPTER IV

BIM ROCHESTER

I

This is the story of Bim Rochester's first Odyssey. It is a story
that has Bim himself for the only proof of its veracity, but he
has never, by a shadow of a word, faltered in his account of it,
and has remained so unamazed at some of the strange aspects
in it that it seems almost an impertinence that we ourselves
should show any wonder. Benjamin (Bim) Rochester was
probably the happiest little boy in March Square, and he was
happy in spite of quite a number of disadvantages.

A word about the Rochester family is here necessary. They
inhabited the largest house in March Square—the large grey
one at the corner by Lent Street—and yet it could not be said
to be large enough for them. Mrs. Rochester was a black-
haired woman with flaming cheeks and a most untidy
appearance. Her mother had been a Spaniard, and her father
an English artist, and she was very much the child of both of
them. Her hair was always coming down, her dress unfastened,
her shoes untied, her boots unbuttoned. She rushed through
life with an amazing shattering vigour, bearing children,
flinging them into an already overcrowded nursery, rushing
out to parties, filling the house with crowds of friends,
acquaintances, strangers, laughing, chattering, singing, never
out of temper, never serious, never, for a moment, to be
depended on. Her husband, a grave, ball-faced man, spent

most of his days in the City and at his club, but was fond of his wife, and admired what he called her "energy." "My wife's splendid," he would say to his friends, "knows the whole of London, I believe. The *people* we have in our house!" He would watch, sometimes, the strange, noisy parties, and then would retire to bridge at his club with a little sigh of pride.

Meanwhile, upstairs in the nursery there were children of all ages, and two nurses did their best to grapple with them. The nurses came and went, and always, after the first day or two, the new nurse would give in to the conditions, and would lead, at first with amusement and a rather excited sense of adventure, afterwards with a growing feeling of dirt and discomfort, a tangled and helter-skelter existence. Some of the children were now at school, but Lucy, a girl ten years of age, was a supercilious child who rebelled against the conditions of her life, but was too idle and superior to attempt any alteration of them. After her there were Roger, Dorothy, and Robert. Then came Bim, four years of age a fortnight ago, and, last of all, Timothy, an infant of nine months. With the exception of Lucy and Bim they were exceedingly noisy children. Lucy should have passed her days in the schoolroom under the care of Miss Agg, a melancholy and hope-abandoned spinster, and, during lesson hours, there indeed she was. But in the schoolroom she had no one to impress with her amazing wisdom and dignity. "Poor mummy," as she always thought of her mother, was quite unaware of her habits or movements, and Miss Agg was unable to restrain either the one or the other, so Lucy spent most of her time in the nursery, where she sat, calm and collected, in the midst of confusion that could have "given old Babel points and won easy." She was reverenced by all the younger children for her sedate security, but by none of them so surely and so magnificently as Bim. Bim, because he was quieter than the other children, claimed for his opinions and movements the stronger interest.

His nurses called him "deep," "although for a deep child I must say he's 'appy."

Hugh Walpole

Both his depth and his happiness were at Lucy's complete disposal. The people who saw him in the Square called him "a jolly little boy," and, indeed, his appearance of gravity was undermined by the curl of his upper lip and a dimple in the middle of his left cheek, so that he seemed to be always at the crisis of a prolonged chuckle. One very rarely heard him laugh out loud, and his sturdy, rather fat body was carried rather gravely, and he walked contemplatively as though he were thinking something out. He would look at you, too, very earnestly when you spoke to him, and would wait a little before he answered you, and then would speak slowly as though he were choosing his words with care. And yet he was, in spite of these things, really a "jolly little boy." His "jolliness" was there in point of view, in the astounding interest he found in anything and everything, in his refusal to be upset by any sort of thing whatever.

But his really unusual quality was his mixture of stolid English matter-of-fact with an absolutely unbridled imagination. He would pursue, day by day, week after week, games, invented games of his own, that owed nothing, either for their inception or their execution, to any one else. They had their origin for the most part in stray sentences that he had overheard from his elders, but they also arose from his own private and personal experiences—experiences which were as real to him as going to the dentist or going to the pantomime were to his brothers and sisters. There was, for instance, a gentleman of whom he always spoke of as Mr. Jack. This friend no one had ever seen, but Bim quoted him frequently. He did not, apparently, see him very often now, but at one time when he had been quite a baby Mr. Jack had been always there. Bim explained, to any one who cared to listen, that Mr. Jack belonged to all the Other Time which he was now in very serious danger of forgetting, and when, at that point, he was asked with condescending indulgence, "I suppose you mean fairies, dear!" he always shook his head scornfully and said he meant nothing of the kind, Mr. Jack was as real as mother, and, indeed, a great deal "realer," because Mrs. Rochester was, in the course of her energetic career, able to devote only "whirlwind" visits to her "dear, darling" children.

When the afternoon was spent in the gardens in the middle of the Square, Bim would detach himself from his family and would be found absorbed in some business of his own which he generally described as "waiting for Mr. Jack."

"Not the sort of child," said Miss Agg, who had strong views about children being educated according to practical and common-sense ideas, "not the sort of child that one would expect nonsense from." It may be quite safely asserted that never, in her very earliest years, had Miss Agg been guilty of any nonsense of the sort.

But it was not Miss Agg's contempt for his experiences that worried Bim. He always regarded that lady with an amused indifference. "She *bothers* so," he said once to Lucy. "Do you think she's happy with us, Lucy?"

"P'r'aps. I'm sure it doesn't matter."

"I suppose she'd go away if she wasn't," he concluded, and thought no more about her.

No, the real grief in his heart was that Lucy, the adored, the wonderful Lucy, treated his assertions with contempt.

"But, Bim, don't be such a silly baby. You know you can't have seen him. Nurse was there and a lot of us, and *we* didn't."

"I did though."

"But, Bim—"

"Can't help it. He used to come lots and lots."

"You *are* a silly! You're getting too old now—"

"I'm *not* a silly!"

"Yes, you are."

"I'm not!"

"Oh, well, of course, if you're going to be a naughty baby."

Bim was nearer tears on these occasions than on any other in all his mortal life. His adoration of Lucy was the foundation-stone of his existence, and she accepted it with a lofty assumption of indifference; but very sharply would she have missed it had it been taken from her, and in long after years she was to look back upon that love of his and wonder that she could have accepted it so lightly; Bim found in her gravity and assurance all that he demanded of his elders. Lucy was never at a loss for an answer to any question, and Bim believed all that she told him.

"Where's China, Lucy?'

"Oh, don't bother, Bim."

"No, but *where* is it?"

"What a nuisance you are! It's near Africa."

"Where Uncle Alfred is?"

"Yes, just there."

"But *is* Uncle Alfred in—China?"

"No, silly, of course not."

"Well, then—"

"I didn't say China was in Africa. I said it was near."

"Oh! I see. Uncle Alfred could just go in the train?"

"Yes, of course."

"Oh! I see. P'r'aps he will."

But, for the most part, Bim, realising that Lucy "didn't want to be bothered," pursued his life alone. Through all the turmoil and disorder of that tempestuous nursery he gravely went his way, at one moment fighting lions and tigers, at another being nurse on her afternoon out (this was a truly astonishing adventure composed of scraps flung to him from nurse's conversational table and including many incidents that were far indeed from any nurse's experience), or again, he would be his mother giving a party, and, in the course of this, a great deal of food would be eaten, his favourite dishes, treacle pudding and cottage pie, being always included.

With the exception of his enthusiasm for Lucy he was no sentimentalist. He hated being kissed, he did not care very greatly for Roger and Dorothy and Robert, and regarded them as nothing but nuisances when they interfered with his games or compelled him to join in theirs.

And now this is the story of his Odyssey.

II

It happened on a wet April afternoon. The morning had been fine, a golden morning with the scent in the air of the showers that had fallen during the night. Then, suddenly, after midday, the rain came down, splashing on to the shining pavements as it fell, beating on to the windows and then running, in little lines, on to the ledges and falling from there in slow, heavy drops. The sky was black, the statues in the garden dejected, the almond tree beaten, all the little paths running with water, and on the garden seats the rain danced like a live thing.

The children—Lucy, Roger, Dorothy, Robert, Bim, and Timothy—were, of course, in the nursery. The nurse was toasting her toes on the fender and enjoying immensely that story by Mrs. Henry Wood, entitled "The Shadow of Ashlydyat." It is entirely impossible to present any adequate idea of the confusion and bizarrerie of that nursery. One must think of the most confused aspect of human life that one has ever known—say, a Suffrage attack upon the Houses of Parliament, or a Channel steamer on a Thursday morning, and then of the next most confused aspect. Then one must place them together and confess defeat. Mrs. Rochester was not, as I have said, very frequently to be found in her children's nursery, but she managed, nevertheless, to pervade the house, from cellar to garret, with her spirit. Toys were everywhere—dolls and trains and soldiers, bricks and puzzles and animals, cardboard boxes, articles of feminine attire, a zinc bath, two cats, a cage with white mice, a pile of books resting in a dazzling pyramid on the very edge of the table, two glass jars containing minute fish of the new variety, and a bowl with goldfish. There were many other things, forgotten by me.

Lucy, her pigtails neatly arranged, sat near the window and pretended to be reading that fascinating story, "The Pillars of the House." I say pretending, because Lucy did not care about reading at any time, and especially disliked the works of Charlotte Mary Yonge, but she thought that it looked well that she and nurse should be engaged upon literature whilst the rest of the world rioted and gambolled their time away. There was no one who at the moment could watch and admire her fine spirit, but you never knew who might come in.

The rioting and gambolling consisted in the attempts of Robert, Dorothy, and Roger, to give a realistic presentation to an audience of one, namely, the infant Timothy, of the life of the Red Indians and their Squaws. Underneath the nursery table, with a tablecloth, some chairs and a concertina, they were presenting an admirable and entirely engrossing performance.

Bim, under the window and quite close to Lucy, was giving a party. He had possessed himself of some of Dorothy's dolls' tea things, he had begged a sponge cake from nurse, and could be heard breaking from time to time into such sentences as, "Do have a little more tweacle pudding, Mrs. Smith. It's the best tweacle," and, "It's a nice day, isn't it!" but he was sorely interrupted by the noisy festivities of the Indians who broke, frequently, into realistic cries of "Oh! Roger, you're pulling my hair," or "I won't play if you don't look out!"

It may be that these interruptions disturbed the actuality of Bim's festivities, or it may be that the rattling of the rain upon the window panes diverted his attention. Once he broke into a chuckle. "Isn't they banging on the window, Lucy?" he said, but she was, it appeared, too deeply engaged to answer him. He found that, in a moment of abstraction, he had eaten the whole of the sponge cake, so that it was obvious that the party was over. "Good-bye, Mrs. Smith. It was really nice of you to come. Good-bye, dear, Mrs. — I think the wain almost isn't coming now."

He said farewell to them all and climbed upon the window seat. Here, gazing down into the Square, he saw that the rain was stopping, and, on the farther side, above the roofs of the houses, a little splash of gold had crept into the grey. He watched the gold, heard the rain coming more slowly; at first, "spatter-spatter-spatter," then, "spatter—spatter." Then one drop very slowly after another drop. Then he saw that the sun from somewhere far away had found out the wet paths in the garden, and was now stealing, very secretly, along them. Soon it would strike the seat, and then the statue of the funny fat man in all his clothes, and then, perhaps, the fountain. He was unhappy a little, and he did not know why: he was conscious, perhaps, of the untidy, noisy room behind him, of his sister Dorothy who, now a Squaw of a quite genuine and realistic kind, was crying at the top of her voice: "I don't care. I will have it if I want to. You're *not* to, Roger," and of Timothy, his baby brother, who, moved by his sister's cries, howled monotonously, persistently, hopelessly.

"Oh, give over, do, Miss Dorothy!" said the nurse, raising her eye for a moment from her book. "Why can't you be quiet?"

Outside the world was beginning to shine and glitter, inside it was all horrid and noisy. He sighed a little, he wanted to express in some way his feelings. He looked at Lucy and drew closer to her. She had beside her a painted china mug which one of her uncles had brought her from Russia; she had stolen some daffodils from her mother's room downstairs and now was arranging them. This painted mug was one of her most valued possessions, and Bim himself thought it, with its strange red and brown figures running round it, the finest thing in all the world.

"Lucy," he said. "Do you s'pose if you was going to jump all the way down to the street and wasn't afraid that p'r'aps your legs wouldn't get broken?"

He was not, in reality, greatly interested in the answer to his question, but the important thing always with Lucy was first to enchain her attention. He had learnt, long ago, that to tell her that he loved her, to invite tenderness from her in return, was to ask for certain rebuff—he always began his advances then in this roundabout manner.

"*What do* you think, Lucy?"

"Oh, I don't know. How can I tell? Don't bother."

It was then that Bim felt what was, for him, a very rare sensation. He was irritated.

"I don't bovver," he said, with a cross look in the direction of his brother and sister Rochesters. "No, but, Lucy, s'pose some one—nurse, s'pose—*did* fall down into the street and broke all her legs and arms, she wouldn't be dead, would she?"

"You silly little boy, of course not."

He looked at Lucy, saw the frown upon her forehead, and felt suddenly that all his devotion to her was wasted, that she didn't want him, that nobody wanted him—now when the sun was making the garden glitter like a jewel and the fountain to shine like a sword.

He felt in his throat a hard, choking lump. He came closer to his sister.

"You might pay 'tention, Lucy," he said plaintively.

Lucy broke a daffodil stalk viciously. "Go and talk to the others," she said. "I haven't time for you."

The tears were hot in his eyes and anger was in his heart— anger bred of the rain, of the noise, of the confusion.

"You *are* howwid," he said slowly.

"Well, go away, then, if I'm horrid," she pushed with her hand at his knee. "I didn't ask you to come here."

Her touch infuriated him; he kicked and caught a very tender part of her calf.

"Oh! You little beast!" She came to him, leant for a moment across him, then slapped his cheek.

The pain, the indignity, and, above all, a strange confused love for his sister that was near to passionate rage, let loose all the devils that owned Bim for their habitation.

He did three things: He screamed aloud, he bent forward and bit Lucy's hand hard, he seized Lucy's wonderful Russian mug and dashed it to the ground. He then stood staring at the shattered fragments.

III

There followed, of course, confusion. Nurse started up. "The Shadow of Ashlydyat" descended into the ashes, the children rushed eagerly from beneath the table to the centre of hostilities.

But there were no hostilities. Lucy and Bim were, both of them, utterly astonished, Lucy, as she looked at the scattered mug, was, indeed, sobbing, but absent-mindedly—her thoughts were elsewhere. Her thoughts, in fact, were with Bim. She realised suddenly that never before had he lost his temper with her; she was aware that his affection had been all this time of value to her, of much more value, indeed, than the stupid old mug. She bent down—still absent-mindedly sobbing—and began to pick up the pieces. She was really astonished—being a dry and rather hard little girl—at her affection for Bim.

The nurse seized on the unresisting villain of the piece and shook him. "You *naughty* little boy! To go and break your sister's beautiful mug. It's your horrid temper that'll be the ruin of you, mark my words, as I'm always telling you." (Bim had never been known to lose his temper before.) "Yes, it will. You see, you naughty boy. And all the other children as good as gold and quiet as lambs, and you've got to go and do this. You shall stand in the corner all tea-time, and not a bite shall you have." Here Bim began, in a breathless, frightened way, to sob. "Yes, well you may. Never mind, Miss Lucy, I dare say your uncle will bring you another." Here she became conscious of an attentive and deeply interested audience. "Now, children, time to get ready for tea. Run along, Miss Dorothy, now. What a nuisance you all are, to be sure."

They were removed from the scene. Bim was placed in the corner with his face to the wall. He was aghast; no words can give, at all, any idea of how dumbly aghast he was. What possessed him? What, in an instant of time, had leapt down from the clouds, had sprung up from the Square and seized him? Between his amazed thoughts came little surprised sobs.

But he had not abandoned himself to grief—he was too sternly set upon the problem of reparation. Something must be done, and that quickly.

The great thought in his mind was that he must replace the mug. He had not been very often in the streets beyond the Square, but upon certain occasions he had seen their glories, and he knew that there had been shops and shops and shops. Quite close to him, upon a shelf, was his money-box, a squat, ugly affair of red tin, into whose large mouth he had been compelled to force those gifts that kind relations had bestowed. There must be now quite a fortune there—enough to buy many mugs. He could not himself open it, but he did not doubt that the man in the shop would do that for him.

Not for many more moments would he be left alone. His hat was lying on the table; he seized that and his money-box, and was out on the landing.

The rest is *his* story. I cannot, as I have already said, vouch for the truth of it. At first, fortune was on his side. There seemed to be no one about the house. He went down the wide staircase without making any sound; in the hall he stopped for a moment because he heard voices, but no one came. Then with both hands, and standing on tiptoe, he turned the lock of the door, and was outside.

The Square was bathed in golden sun, a sun, the stronger for his concealment, but tempered, too, with the fine gleam that the rain had left. Never before had Bim been outside that door alone; he was aware that this was a very tremendous adventure. The sky was a washed and delicate purple, and behold! on the high railings, a row of sparrows were chattering. Voices were cold and clear, echoing, as it seemed, against the straight, grey walls of the houses, and all the trees in the garden glistened with their wet leaves shining with gold; there seemed to be, too, a dim veil of smoke that was homely and comfortable.

It is not usual to see a small boy of four alone in a London square, but Bim met, at first, no one except a messenger boy, who stopped and looked after him. At the corner of the Square—just out of the Square so that it might not shame its grandeur—was a fruit and flower shop, and this shop was the entrance to a street that had much life and bustle about it. Here Bim paused with his money-box clasped very tightly to him. Then he made a step or two and was instantly engulfed, it seemed, in a perfect whirl of men and women, of carts and bicycles, of voices and cries and screams; there were lights of every colour, and especially one far above his head that came and disappeared and came again with terrifying wizardry.

He was, quite suddenly, and as it were, by the agency of some outside person, desperately frightened. It was a new terror, different from anything that he had known before. It was as though a huge giant had suddenly lifted him up by the seat of his breeches, or a witch had transplanted him on to her broomstick and carried him off. It was as unusual as that.

His under lip began to quiver, and he knew that presently he would be crying. Then, as he always did, when something unusual occurred to him, he thought of "Mr. Jack." At this point, when you ask him what happened, he always says: "Oh! He came, you know—came walking along—like he always did."

"Was he just like other people, Bim?"

"Yes, just. With a beard, you know—just like he always was."

"Yes, but what sort of things did he wear?" "Oh, just ord'nary things, like you." There was no sense of excitement or wonder to be got out of him. It was true that Mr. Jack hadn't shown himself for quite a long time, but that, Bim felt, was natural enough. "He'll come less and seldomer and seldomer as you get big, you know. It was just at first, when one was very little and didn't know one's way about—just to help babies not to be frightened. Timothy would tell you only he won't. Then he comes only a little—just at special times like this was."

Bim told you this with a slightly bored air, as though it were silly of you not to know, and really his air of certainty made an incredulous challenge a difficult thing. On the present occasion Mr. Jack was just there, in the middle of the crowd, smiling and friendly. He took Bim's hand, and, "Of course," Bim said, "there didn't have to be any 'splaining. *He* knew what I wanted." True or not, I like to think of them, in the evening air, serenely safe and comfortable, and in any case, it was surely strange that if, as one's common sense compels one to suppose, Bim were all alone in that crowd, no one wondered or stopped him nor asked him where his home was. At any rate, I have no opinions on the subject. Bim says that, at once, they found themselves out of the crowd in a quiet, little "dinky" street, as he called it, a street that, in his description of it, answered to nothing that I can remember in this part of the world. His account of it seems to present a dark, rather narrow place, with overhanging roofs and swinging signs, and nobody, he says, at all about, but a church with a bell, and outside one shop a row of bright-coloured clothes hanging. At any rate, here Bim found the place that he wanted. There was a little shop with steps down into it and a tinkling bell which made a tremendous noise when you pushed the old oak door. Inside there was every sort of thing. Bim lost himself here in the ecstasy of his description, lacking also names for many of the things that he saw. But there was a whole suit of shining armour, and there were jewels, and old brass trays, and carpets, and a crocodile, which Bim called a "crodocile." There was also a friendly old man with a white beard, and over everything a lovely smell, which Bim said was like "roast potatoes" and "the stuff mother has in a bottle in her bedwoom."

Bim could, of course, have stayed there for ever, but Mr. Jack reminded him of a possibly anxious family. "There, is that what you're after?" he said, and, sure enough, there on a shelf, smiling and eager to be bought, was a mug exactly like the one that Bim had broken.

There was then the business of paying for it, the money-box

Hugh Walpole

was produced and opened by the old man with "a shining knife," and Bim was gravely informed that the money found in the box was exactly the right amount. Bim had been, for a moment, in an agony of agitation lest he should have too little, but as he told us, "There was all Uncle Alfred's Christmas money, and what mother gave me for the tooth, and that silly lady with the green dress who *would* kiss me." So, you see, there must have been an awful amount.

Then they went, Bim clasping his money-box in one hand and the mug in the other. The mug was wrapped in beautiful blue paper that smelt, as we were all afterwards to testify, of dates and spices. The crocodile flapped against the wall, the bell tinkled, and the shop was left behind them. "Most at once," Bim said they were by the fruit shop again; he knew that Mr. Jack was going, and he had a sudden most urgent longing to go with him, to stay with him, to be with him always. He wanted to cry; he felt dreadfully unhappy, but all of his thanks, his strange desires, that he could bring out was, in a quavering voice, trying hard, you understand, not to cry, "Mr. Jack. Oh! Mr.—" and his friend was gone.

IV

He trotted home; with every step his pride increased. What would Lucy say? And dim, unrealised, but forming, nevertheless, the basis for the whole of his triumph, was his consciousness that she who had scoffed, derided, at his "Mr. Jack," should now so absolutely benefit by him. This was bringing together, at last, the two of them.

His nurse, in a fine frenzy of agitation, met him. Her relief at his safety swallowed her anger. She could only gasp at him. "Well, Master Bim, and a nice state— Oh, dear! to think; wherever—"

On the doorstep he forced his nurse to pause, and, turning, looked at the gardens now in shadow of spun gold, with the fountain blue as the sky. He nodded his head with satisfaction. It had been a splendid time. It would be a very long while, he knew, before he was allowed out again like that. Yes. He clasped the mug tightly, and the door closed behind him.

I don't know that there is anything more to say. There were the empty money-box and the mug. There was Bim's unhesitating and unchangeable story. There *is* a shop, just behind the Square, where they have some Russian crockery. But Bim alone!

I don't know.

CHAPTER V

NANCY ROSS

I

Mr. Munty Ross's house was certainly the smartest in March
Square; No. 14, where the Duchess of Crole lived, was shabby
in comparison. Very often you may see a line of motor-cars
and carriages stretching down the Square, then round the
corner into Lent Street, and you may know then—as, indeed,
all the Square did know and most carefully observed—that
Mrs. Munty Boss was giving another of her smart little parties.
That dark-green door, that neat overhanging balcony, those
rows—in the summer months—of scarlet geraniums, that roll
of carpet that ran, many times a week, from the door over the
pavement to the very foot of the waiting vehicle—these things
were Mrs. Munty Ross s.

Munty Ross—a silent, ugly, black little man—had had made
his money in potted shrimps, or something equally compact
and indigestible, and it really was very nice to think that
anything in time could blossom out into beauty as striking as
Mrs. Munty's lovely dresses, or melody as wonderful as the
voice of M. Radiziwill, the famous tenor, whom she often
"turned on" at her little evening parties. Upon Mr. Munty
alone the shrimps seemed to have made no effect. He was as
black, as insignificant, as ugly as ever he had been in the days
before he knew of a shrimp's possibilities. He was very silent at
his wife's parties, and sometimes dropped his h's. What Mrs.

Munty had been before her marriage no one quite knew, but now she was flaxen and slim and beautifully clothed, with a voice like an insincere canary; she had "a passion for the Opera," a "passion for motoring," "a passion for the latest religion," and "a passion for the simple life." All these things did the shrimps enable her to gratify, and "the simple life" cost her more than all the others put together.

Heaven had blessed them with one child, and that child was called Nancy. Nancy, her mother always said with pride, was old for her age, and, as her age was only just five, that remark was quite true. Nancy Ross was old for any age. Had she herself, one is compelled when considering her to wonder, any conception during those first months of the things that were going to be made out of her, and had she, perhaps at the very commencement of it all, some instinct of protest and rebellion? Poor Nancy! The tragedy of her whole case was now none other than that she hadn't, here at five years old in March Square, the slightest picture of what she had become, nor could she, I suppose, have imagined it possible for her to become anything different. Nancy, in her own real and naked person, was a small child with a good flow of flaxen hair and light-blue eyes. All her features were small and delicate, and she gave you the impression that if you only pulled a string or pushed a button somewhere in the middle of her back you could evoke any cry, smile or exclamation that you cared to arouse. Her eyes were old and weary, her attitude always that of one who had learnt the ways of this world, had found them sawdust, but had nevertheless consented still to play the game. Just as the house was filled with little gilt chairs and china cockatoos, so was Nancy arrayed in ribbons and bows and lace. Mrs. Munty had, one must suppose, surveyed during certain periods in her life certain real emotions rather as the gaping villagers survey the tiger behind his bars in the travelling circus.

The time had then come when she put these emotions away from her as childish things, and determined never to be faced with any of them again. It was not likely, then, that she would introduce Nancy to any of them. She introduced Nancy to clothes and deportment, and left it at that. She wanted her child to "look nice." She was able, now that Nancy was five years old, to say that she "looked very nice indeed."

II

From the very beginning nurses were chosen who would take care of Nancy Boss's appearance. There was plenty of money to spend, and Nancy was a child who, with her flaxen hair and blue eyes, would repay trouble. She *did* repay it, because she had no desires towards grubbiness or rebellion, or any wildnesses whatever. She just sat there with her doll balanced neatly in her arms, and allowed herself to be pulled and twisted and squeezed and stretched. "There's a pretty little lady," said nurse, and a pretty little lady Nancy was sure that she was. The order for her day was that in the morning she went out for a walk in the gardens in the Square, and in the afternoon she went out for another. During these walks she moved slowly, her doll delicately carried, her beautiful clothes shining with approval of the way that they were worn, her head high, "like a little queen," said her nurse. She was conscious of the other children in the gardens, who often stopped in the middle of their play and watched her. She thought them hot and dirty and very noisy. She was sorry for their mothers.

It happened sometimes that she came downstairs, towards the end of a luncheon party, and was introduced to the guests. "You pretty little thing," women in very large hats said to her. "Lovely hair," or "She's the very image of *you*, Clarice," to her mother. She liked to hear that because she greatly admired her mother. She knew that she, Nancy Ross, was beautiful; she knew that clothes were of an immense importance; she knew that other children were unpleasant. For the rest, she was neither extravagantly glad nor extravagantly sorry. She preserved a fine indifference.... And yet, although, here my story may seem to matter-of-fact persons to take a turn towards the fantastic, this was not quite all. Nancy herself, dimly and yet uneasily, was aware that there was something else.

She was not a little girl who believed in fairies or witches or the "bogey man," or anything indeed that she could not see. She inherited from her mother a splendid confidence in the reality, the solid, unquestioned reality of all concrete and tangible things. She had been presented once with a fine edition of "Grimm's Fairy Tales," an edition with coloured pictures and every allure. She had turned its pages with a look of incredulous amazement. "What," she seemed to say—she was then aged three and a half—"are these absurd things that you are telling me? People aren't like that. Mother isn't in the least like that. I don't understand this, and it's tedious!"

"I'm afraid the child has no imagination," said her nurse.

"What a lucky thing!" said her mother.

Nor could Mrs. Ross's house be said to be a place that encouraged fairies. They would have found the gilt chairs hard to sit upon, and there were no mysterious corners. There was nothing mysterious at all. And yet Nancy Ross, sitting in her magnificent clothes, was conscious as she advanced towards her sixth year that she was not perfectly comfortable. To say that she felt lonely would be, perhaps, to emphasise too strongly her discomfort. It was perhaps rather that she felt inquisitive—only a little, a very little—but she did begin to wish that she could ask a few questions.

There came a day—an astonishing day—when she felt irritated with her mother. She had during her walk through the garden seen a little boy and a little girl, who were grubbing about in a little pile of earth and sand there in the corner under the trees, and grubbing very happily. They had dirt upon their faces, but their nurse was sitting, apparently quite easy in her mind, and the sun had not stopped in its course nor had the birds upon the trees ceased to sing. Nancy stayed for a moment her progress and looked at them, and something not very far from envy struck, in some far-distant hiding-place, her soul. She moved on, but when she came indoors and was met by her mamma and a handsome lady, her mamma's friend, who said: "Isn't she a pretty dear?" and her mother said: "That's right, Nancy darling, been for your walk?" she was, for an amazing moment, irritated with her beautiful mother.

III

Once she was conscious of this desire to ask questions she had no more peace. Although she was only five years of age, she had all the determination not "to give herself away" of a woman of forty. She was not going to show that she wanted anything in the world, and yet she would have liked—A little wistfully she looked at her nurse. But that good woman, carefully chosen by Mrs. Ross, was not the one to encourage questions. She was as shining as a new brass nail, and a great deal harder.

The nursery was as neat as a pin, with a lovely bright rocking-horse upon which Nancy had never ridden; a pink doll's-house with every modern contrivance, whose doors had never been opened; a number of expensive dolls, which had never been disrobed. Nancy approached these joys—diffidently and with caution. She rode upon the horse, opened the doll's-house, embraced the dolls, but she had no natural imagination to bestow upon them, and the horse and the dolls, hurt, perhaps, at their long neglect, received her with frigidity. Those grubby little children in the Square would, she knew, have been "there" in a moment. She began then to be frightened. The nursery, her bedroom, the dark little passage outside, were suddenly alarming. Sometimes, when she was sitting quietly in her nursery, the house was so silent that she could have screamed.

"I don't think Miss Nancy's quite well, ma'am," said the nurse.

"Oh, dear! What a nuisance," said Mrs. Ross who liked her little girl to be always well and beautiful. "I do hope she's not going to catch something."

"She doesn't take that pleasure in her clothes she did," said the nurse.

"Perhaps she wants some new ones," said her mother. "Take her to Florice, nurse." Nancy went to Florice, and beautiful new garments were invented, and once again she was squeezed, and tightened, and stretched, and pulled. But Nancy was indifferent. As they tried these clothes, and stood back, and stepped forward, and admired and criticised, she was thinking, "I wish the nursery clock didn't make such a noise."

Her little bedroom next to nurse's large one was a beautiful affair, with red roses up and down the wall-paper and in and out of the crockery and round and round the carpet. Her bed was magnificent, with lace and more roses, and there was a fine photograph of her beautiful mother in a silver frame on the mantelpiece. But all these things were of little avail when the dark came. She began to be frightened of the dark.

There came a night when, waking with a suddenness that did of itself contribute to her alarm, she was conscious that the room was intensely dark, and that every one was very far away. The house, as she listened, seemed to be holding its breath, the clock in the nursery was ticking in a frightened, startled terror, and hesitating, whimsical noises broke, now close, now distant, upon the silence. She lay there, her heart beating as it had surely never been allowed to beat before. She was simply a very small, very frightened little girl. Then, before she could cry out, she was aware that some one was standing beside her bed. She was aware of this before she looked, and then, strangely (even now she had taken no peep), she was frightened no longer.

The room, the house, were suddenly comfortable and safe places; as water slips from a pool and leaves it dry, so had terror glided from her side. She looked up then, and, although the place had been so dark that she had been unable to distinguish the furniture, she could figure to herself quite clearly her visitor's form. She not only figured it, but also quite easily and readily recognised it. All these years she had forgotten him, but now at the vision of his large comfortable presence she was back again amongst experiences and recognitions that evoked for her once more all those odd first days when, with how much discomfort and puzzled dismay, she had been dropped, so suddenly, into this distressing world. He put his arms around her and held her; he bent down and kissed her, and her small hand went up to his beard in exactly the way that it used to do. She nestled up against him.

"It's a very long time, isn't it," he said, "since I paid you a visit!"

"Yes, a long, long time.'

"That's because you didn't want me. You got on so well without me."

"I didn't forget about you," she said. "But I asked mummy about you once, and she said you were all nonsense, and I wasn't to think things like that."

"Ah! your mother's forgotten altogether. She knew me once, but she hasn't wanted me for a very, very long time. She'll see me again, though, one day."

"I'm so glad you've come. You won't go away again now, will you?"

"I never go away," he said. "I'm always here. I've seen everything you've been doing, and a very dull time you've been making of it."

He talked to her and told her about some of the things the other children in the Square were doing. She was interested a little, but not very much; she still thought a great deal more about herself than about anything or anybody else.

"Do they all love you?" she said.

"Oh, no, not at all. Some of them think I'm horrid. Some of them forget me altogether, and then I never come back, until just at the end. Some of them only want me when they're in trouble. Some, very soon, think it silly to believe in me at all, and the older they grow the less they believe, generally. And when I do come they won't see me, they make up their minds not to. But I'm always there just the same; it makes no difference what they do. They can't help themselves. Only it's better for them just to remember me a little, because then it's much safer for them. You've been feeling rather lonely lately, haven't you?"

"Yes," she said. "It's stupid now all by myself. There's nobody to ask questions of."

"Well, there's somebody else in your house who's lonely."

"Is there?" She couldn't think of any one.

"Yes. Your father."

"Oh! Father—" She was uninterested.

"Yes. You see, if he isn't—" and then, at that, he was gone, she was alone and fast asleep.

In the morning when she awoke, she remembered it all quite clearly, but, of course, it had all been a dream. "Such a funny dream," she told her nurse, but she would give out no details.

"Some food she's been eating," said her nurse.

Nevertheless, when, on that afternoon, coming in from her walk, she met her dark, grubby little father in the hall, she did stay for a moment on the bottom step of the stairs to consider him.

"I've been for a walk, daddy," she said, and then, rather frightened at her boldness, tumbled up on the next step. He went forward to catch her.

"Hold up," he said, held her for a moment, and then hurried, confused and rather agitated, into his dark sanctum. These were, very nearly, the first words that they had ever, in the course of their lives together, interchanged. Munty Ross was uneasy with grown-up persons (unless he was discussing business with them), but that discomfort was nothing to the uneasiness that he felt with children. Little girls (who certainly looked at him as though he were an ogre) frightened him quite horribly; moreover, Mrs. Munty had, for a great number of years, pursued a policy with regard to her husband that was not calculated to make him bright and easy in any society. "Poor old Munty," she would say to her friends, "it's not all his fault—" It was, as a fact, very largely hers. He had never been an eloquent man, but her playful derision of his uncouthness slew any little seeds cf polite conversation that might, under happier conditions, have grown into brilliant blossom. It had been understood from the very beginning that Nancy was not of her father's world. He would have been scarcely aware that he had a daughter had he not, at certain periods, paid bills for her clothes.

"What's a child want with all this?" he had ventured once to say.

"Hardly your business, my dear," his wife had told him. "The child's clothes are marvellously cheap considering. I don't know how Florice does it for the money." He resented nothing—it was not his way—but he did feel, deep down in his heart, that the child was over-dressed, that it must be bad for any little girl to be praised in the way that his daughter was praised, that "the kid will grow up with the most tremendous ideas."

He resented it, perhaps a little, that his young daughter had so easily accustomed herself to the thought that she had no father.

"She might just want to see me occasionally. But I'd only frighten her, I suppose, if she did."

Munty Ross had very little of the sentimentalist about him; he was completely cynical about the value of the human heart, and believed in the worth and goodness of no one at all. He had, for a brief wild moment, been in love with his wife, but she had taken care to kill that, "the earlier the better." "My dear," she would say to a chosen friend, "what Munty's like when he's romantic!" She never, after the first month of their married life together, caught a glimpse of that side of him.

Now, however, he did permit his mind to linger over that vision of his little daughter tumbling on the stairs. He wondered what had made her do it. He was astonished at the difference that it made to him.

To Nancy also it had made a great difference. She wished that she had stayed there on the stairs a little longer to hold a more important conversation. She had thought of her father as "all horrid"—now his very contrast to her little world pleased and interested her. It may also be that, although she was young, she had even now a picture in her mind of her father's loneliness. She may have seen into her mother's attitude with an acuteness much older than her actual years.

She thought now continually about her father. She made little plans to meet him, but these meetings were not, as a rule, successful, because so often he was down in the city. She would wait at the end of her afternoon walk on the stairs.

"Come along, Miss Nancy, do. What are you hanging about there for?"

"Nothing."

"You'll be disturbing your mother."

"Just a minute."

Hugh Walpole

She peered anxiously, her little head almost held by the railings of the banisters; she gazed down into black, mysterious depths wherein her father might be hidden. She was driven to all this partly by some real affection that had hitherto found no outlet, partly by a desire for adventure, but partly, also, by some force that was behind her and quite recognised by her. It was as though she said: "If I'm nice to my father and make friends with him, then you must promise that I shan't be frightened in the middle of the night, that the clock won't tick too loudly, that the blind won't flap, that it won't all be too dark and dreadful." She knew that she had made this compact.

Then she had several little encounters with her father. She met him one day on the doorstep. He had come up whilst she was standing there.

"Had a good walk?" he said nervously. She looked at him and laughed. Then he went hurriedly indoors.

On the second occasion she had come down to be shown off at a luncheon party. She had been praised and petted, and then, in the hall, had run into her father's arms. He was in his top-hat, going down to his old city, looking, the nurse thought, "just like a monkey." But Nancy stayed, holding on to the leg of his trousers. Suddenly he bent down and whispered:

"Were they nice to you in there?"

"Yes. Why weren't you there?"

"I was. I left. Got to go and work."

"What sort of work?"

"Making money for your clothes."

"Take me too."

"Would you like to come?"

"Yes. Take me."

He bent down and kissed her, but, suddenly hearing the voices of the luncheon-party, they separated like conspirators. He crept out of the house.

After that there was no question of their alliance. The sort of affection that most children feel for old, ugly, and battered dolls, Nancy now felt for her father, and the warmth of this affection melted her dried, stubborn little soul, caught her up into visions, wonders, sympathies that had seemed surely denied to her for ever.

"Now sit still, Miss Nancy, while I do up the back."

"Oh, silly old clothes!" said Nancy.

Then one day she declared,

"I want to be dirty like those children in the garden."

"And a nice state your mother would be in!" cried the amazed nurse.

"Father wouldn't," Nancy thought. "Father wouldn't mind."

There came at last the wonderful day when her father penetrated into the nursery. He arrived furtively, very much, it appeared, ashamed of himself and exceedingly shy of the nurse. He did not remain very long. He said very little; a funny picture he had made with his blue face, his black shiny hair, his fat little legs, and his anxious, rather stupid eyes. He sat rather awkwardly in a chair, with Nancy on his knee; he wrung his hair for things to say.

The nurse left them for a moment alone together, and then Nancy whispered:

"Daddy, let's go into the gardens together, you and me; just us—no silly old nurse—one mornin'." (She found the little "g" still a difficulty.)

"Would you like that?" he whispered back. "I don't know I'd be much good in a garden."

"Oh, you'll be all right," she asserted with confidence. "I want to dig."

She'd made up her mind then to that. As Hannibal determined to cross the Alps, as Napoleon set his feet towards Moscow, so did Nancy Ross resolve that she would, in the company of her father, dig in the gardens. She stroked her father's hand, rubbed her head upon his sleeve; exactly as she would have caressed, had she been another little girl, the damaged features of her old rag doll. She was beginning, however, for the first time in her life, to love some one other than herself.

He came, then, quite often to the nursery. He would slip in, stay a moment or two, and slip out again. He brought her presents and sweets which made her ill. And always in the presence of Mrs. Munty they appeared as strangers.

The day came when Nancy achieved her desire—they had their great adventure.

IV

A fine summer morning came, and with it, in a bowler hat, at the nursery door, the hour being about eleven, Mr. Munty Boss.

"I'll take Nancy this morning, nurse," he said, with a strange, choking little "cluck" in his throat. Now, the nurse, although, as I've said, of a shining and superficial appearance, was no fool. She had watched the development of the intrigue; her attitude to the master of the house was composed of pity, patronage, and a rather motherly interest. She did not see how her mistress could avoid her attitude: it was precisely the attitude that she would herself have adopted in that position, but, nevertheless, she was sorry for the man. "So out of it as he is!" Her maternal feelings were uppermost now. "It's nice of the child," she thought, "and him so ugly."

"Of course, sir," she said.

"We shall be back in about an hour." He attempted an easy indifference, was conscious that he failed, and blushed.

He was aware that his wife was out.

He carried off his prize.

The gardens were very full on this lovely summer morning, but Nancy, without any embarrassment or confusion, took charge of the proceedings.

"Where are we going?" he said, gazing rather helplessly about him, feeling extremely shy. There were so many bold children —so many bolder nurses; even the birds on the trees seemed to deride him, and a stumpy fox-terrier puppy stood with its four legs planted wide barking at him.

"Over here," she said without a moment's hesitation, and she dragged him along. She halted at last in a corner of the gardens where was a large, overhanging chestnut and a wooden seat. Here the shouts and cries of the children came more dimly, the splashing of the fountain could be heard like a melodious refrain with a fascinating note of hesitation in it, and the deep green leaves of the tree made a cool, thick covering. "Very nice," he said, and sat down on the seat, tilting his hat back and feeling very happy indeed.

Nancy also was very happy. There, in front of her, was the delightful pile of earth and sand untouched, it seemed. In an instant, regardless of her frock, she was down upon her knees.

"I ought to have a spade," she said.

"You'll make yourself dreadfully dirty, Nancy. Your beautiful frock—" But he had nevertheless the feeling that, after all, he had paid for it, and if he hadn't the right to see it ruined, who had?

"Oh!" she murmured with the ecstasy of one who has abandoned herself, freely and with a glad heart, to all the vices. She dug her hands into the mire, she scattered it about her, she scooped and delved and excavated. It was her intention to build something in the nature of a high, high hill. She patted the surface of the sand, and behold! it was instantly a beautiful shape, very smooth and shining.

It was hot, her hat fell back, her knees were thick with the good brown earth—that once lovely creation of Florice was stained and black.

She then began softly, partly to herself, partly to her father, and partly to that other Friend who had helped her to these splendours, a song of joy and happiness. To the ordinary observer, it might have seemed merely a discordant noise proceeding from a little girl engaged in the making of mud pies. It was, in reality, as the chestnut tree, the birds, the fountain, the flowers, the various small children, even the very earth she played with, understood, a fine offering—thanksgiving and triumphal pæan to the God of Heaven, of the earth, and of the waters that were under the earth.

Munty himself caught the refrain. He was recalled to a day when mud pies had been to him also things of surpassing joy. There was a day when, a naked and very ugly little boy, he had danced beside a mountain burn.

He looked upon his daughter and his daughter looked upon him; they were friends for ever and ever. She rose; her fingers were so sticky with mud that they stood apart; down her right cheek ran a fine black smear; her knees were caked.

"Good heavens!" he exclaimed. She flung herself upon him and kissed him; down his cheek also now a fine smear marked its way.

He looked at his watch—one o'clock. "Good heavens!" he said again. "I say, old girl, we'll have to be going. Mother's got a party." He tried ineffectually to cleanse his daughter's face.

"We'll come back," she cried, looking down triumphantly upon her handiwork.

"We'll have to smuggle you up into the nursery somehow." But he added, "Yes, we'll come again."

V

They hurried home. Very furtively Munty Boss fitted his key into the Yale lock of his fine door. They slipped into the hall. There before them were Mrs. Ross and two of her most splendid friends. Very fine was Munty's wife in a tight-clinging frock of light blue, and wearing upon her head a hat like a waste-paper basket with a blue handle at the back of it; very fine were her two lady friends, clothed also in the tightest of garments, shining and lovely and precious.

"Good God, Munty—and the child!"

It was a terrible moment. Quite unconscious was Munty of the mud that stained his cheek, perfectly tranquil his daughter as she gazed with glowing happiness about her. A terrible moment for Mrs. Ross, an unforgettable one for her friends; nor were they likely to keep the humour of it entirely to themselves.

"Down in a minute. Going up to clean." Smiling, he passed his wife. On the bottom step Nancy chanted:

"We've had the most lovely mornin', daddy and I. We've been

diggin'. We're goin' to dig again. Aren't I dirty, mummy?"

Round the corner of the stairs in the shadow Nancy kissed her father again.

"I'm never goin' to be clean any more," she announced. And you may fancy, if you please, that somewhere in the shadows of the house some one heard those words and chuckled with delighted pleasure.

CHAPTER VI

'ENERY

I

Mrs. Slater was caretaker at No. 21 March. Square. Old Lady Cathcart lived with her middle-aged daughter at No. 21, and, during half the year, they were down at their place in Essex; during half the year, then, Mrs. Slater lived in the basement of No. 21 with her son Henry, aged six.

Mrs. Slater was a widow; upon a certain afternoon, two and a half years ago, she had paused in her ironing and listened. "Something," she told her friends afterwards, "gave her a start—she couldn't say what nor how." Her ironing stayed, for that afternoon at least, where it was, because her husband, with his head in a pulp and his legs bent underneath him, was brought in on a stretcher, attended by two policemen. He had fallen from a piece of scaffolding into Piccadilly Circus, and was unable to afford any further assistance to the improvements demanded by the Pavilion Music Hall. Mrs. Slater, a stout, amiable woman, who had never been one to worry; Henry Slater, Senior, had been a bad husband, "what with women and the drink"—she had no intention of lamenting him now that he was dead; she had done for ever with men, and devoted the whole of her time and energy to providing bread and butter for herself and her son.

She had been Lady Cathcart's caretaker for a year and a half, and had given every satisfaction. When the old lady came up to London Mrs. Slater went down to Essex and defended the country place from suffragettes and burglars. "I shouldn't care for it," said a lady friend, "all alone in the country with no cheerful noises nor human beings."

"Doesn't frighten me, I give you my word, Mrs. East," said Mrs. Slater; "not that I don't prefer the town, mind you."

It was, on the whole, a pleasant life, that carried with it a certain dignity. Nobody who had seen old Lady Cathcart drive in her open carriage, with her black bonnet, her coachman, and her fine, straight back, could deny that she was one of Our Oldest and Best—none of your mushroom families come from Lord knows where—it was a position of trust, and as such Mrs. Slater considered it. For the rest she loved her son Henry with more than a mother's love; he was as unlike his poor father, bless him, as any child could be. Henry, although you would never think it to look at him, was not quite like other children; he had been, from his birth, a "little queer, bless his heart," and Mrs. Slater attributed this to the fact that three weeks before the boy's birth, Horny Slater, Senior, had, in a fine frenzy of inebriation, hit her over the head with a chair. "Dead drunk, 'e was, and never a thought to the child coming, ''Enery,' I said to him, 'it's the child you're hitting as well as me'; but 'e was too far gone, poor soul, to take a thought."

Henry was a fine, robust child, with rosy cheeks and a sturdy, thick-set body. He had large blue eyes and a happy, pleasant smile, but, although he was six years of age, he could hardly talk at all, and liked to spend the days twirling pieces of string round and round or looking into the fire. His eyes were unlike the eyes of other children, and in their blue depths there lurked strange apprehensions, strange anticipations, strange remembrances. He had never, from the day of his birth, been known to cry. When he was frightened or distressed the colour would pass slowly from his cheeks, and strange little gasping breaths would come from him; his body would stiffen and his hands clench. If he was angry the colour in his face would darken and his eyes half close, and it was then that he did, indeed, seem in the possession of some disastrous thraldom— but he was angry very seldom, and only with certain people; for the most part he was a happy child, "as quiet as a mouse." He was unusual, too, in that he was a very cleanly child, and loved to be washed, and took the greatest care of his clothes. He was very affectionate, fond of almost every one, and passionately devoted to his mother.

Mrs. Slater was a woman with very little imagination. She never speculated on "how different things would be if they were different," nor did she sigh after riches, nor possessions, nor any of the goods Fate bestows upon her favourites. She would, most certainly, have been less fond of Henry had he been more like other children, and his dependence upon her gave her something of the feeling that very rich ladies have for very small dogs. She was too, in a way, proud. "Never been able to talk, nor never will, they tell me, the lamb," she would assure her friends, "but as gentle and as quiet!"

She would sit, sometimes, in the evening before the fire and think of the old noisy, tiresome days when Henry, Senior, would beat her black and blue, and would feel that her life had indeed fallen into pleasant places.

There was nothing whatever in the house, all silent about her and filled with shrouded furniture, that could alarm her. "Ghosts!" she would cry. "You show me one, that's all. I'll give you ghosts!"

Her digestion was excellent, her sleep undisturbed by conscience or creditors. She was a happy woman.

Henry loved March Square. There was a window in an upstairs passage from behind whose glass he could gaze at the passing world. The Passing World!... the shrouded house behind him. One was as alive, as bustling, as demonstrative to him as the other, but between the two there was, for him, no communication. His attitude to the Square and the people in it was that he knew more about them than anyone else did; his attitude to the House, that he knew nothing at all compared with what "They" knew. In the Square he could see through the lot of them, so superficial were they all; in the House he could only wait, with fingers on lip, for the next revelation that they might vouchsafe to him.

Doors were, for the most part, locked, yet there were many days when fires were lit because the house was an old one, and damp Lady Cathcart had a horror of.

Always for young Henry the house wore its buried and abandoned air. He was never to see it when the human beings in it would count more than its furniture, and the human life in it more than the house itself. He had come, a year and a half ago, into the very place that his dreams had, from the beginning, built for him. Those large, high rooms with the shining floors, the hooded furniture, the windows gaping without their curtains, the shadows and broad squares of light, the little whispers and rattles that doors and cupboards gave, the swirl of the wind as it sprang released from corners and crevices, the lisp of some whisper, "I'm coming! I'm coming! I'm coming!" that, nevertheless, again and again defeated expectation. How could he but enjoy the fine field of affection that these provided for him?

His mother watched him with maternal pride. "He's *that* contented!" she would say. "Any other child would plague your life away, but 'Enery—"

It was part of Henry's unusual mind that he wondered at nothing. He remained in constant expectation, but whatever was to come to him it would not bring surprise with it. He was in a world where anything might happen. In all the house his favourite room was the high, thin drawing-room with an old gold mirror at one end of it and a piano muffled in brown holland. The mirror caught the piano with its peaked inquiring shape, that, in its inflection, looked so much more tremendous and ominous than it did in plain reality. Through the mirror the piano looked as though it might do anything, and to Henry, who knew nothing about pianos, it was responsible for almost everything that occurred in the house.

The windows of the room gave a fine display of the gardens, the children, the carriages, and the distant houses, but it was when the Square was empty that Henry liked best to gaze down into it, because then the empty house and the empty square prepared themselves together for some tremendous occurrence. Whenever such an interval of silence struck across the noise and traffic of the day, it seemed that all the world screwed itself up for the next event. "One—two—three." But the crisis never came. The noise returned again, people laughed and shouted, bells rang and motors screamed. Nevertheless, one day something would surely happen.

The house was full of company, and the boy would, sometimes, have yielded to the Fear that was never far away, had it not been for some one whom he had known from the very beginning of everything, some one who was as real as his mother, some one who was more powerful than anything or any one in the house, and kinder, far, far kinder.

Often when Mrs. Slater would wonder of what her son was thinking as he sat twisting string round and round in front of the fire, he would be aware of his Friend in the shadow of the light, watching gravely, in the cheerful room, having beneath his hands all the powers, good and evil, of the house. Just as Henry pictured quite clearly to himself other occupants of the house—some one with taloned claws behind the piano, another with black-hooded eyes and a peaked cap in the shadows of an upstairs passage, another brown, shrivelled and naked, who dwelt in a cupboard in one of the empty bedrooms so, too, he could see his Friend, vast and shadowy, with a flowing beard and eyes that were kind and shining.

Often he had felt the pressure of his hand, had heard his reassuring whisper in his ears, had known the touch of his lips upon his forehead. No harm could come to him whilst his

Hugh Walpole

Friend was in the house—and his Friend was always there.

He went always with his mother into the streets when she did her shopping or simply took the air. It was natural that on these occasions, he should be more frightened than during his hours in the house. In the first place his Friend did not accompany him on these out-of-door excursions, and his mother was not nearly so strong a protector as his Friend.

Then he was disturbed by the people who pressed and pushed about him—he had a sense that they were all like birds with flapping wings and strange cries, rushing down upon him— the colours and confusion of the shops bewildered him. There was too much here for him properly to understand; he had enough to do with the piano, the mirror, the shadowed passages, the staring windows.

But in the Square he was happy again. Mrs. Slater never ventured into the gardens; they were for her superiors, and she complacently accepted a world in which things were so ordered as the only world possible. But there was plenty of life outside the gardens.

There were, on the different days of the week, the various musicians, and Henry was friendly with them all. He delighted in music; as he stood there, listening to the barrel-organ, the ideas, pictures, dreams, flew like flocks of beautiful birds through his brain, fleet, and always just beyond his reach, so that he could catch nothing, but would nod his head and would hope that the tune would be repeated, because next time he might, perhaps, be more fortunate.

The Major, who played the harp on Saturdays, was a friend of Mrs. Slater. "Nice little feller, that of yours, mum," he would say. "'Ad one meself once."

"Indeed?"

"Yes, sure enough.... Nice day.... Would you believe it, this is the only London square left for us to play in?... 'Tis, indeed. Cruel shame, I call it; life's 'ard.... You're right, mum, it is. Well, good-day."

Mrs. Slater looked after him affectionately. "Pore feller; and yet I dare say he makes a pretty hit of it if all was known."

Henry sighed. The birds were flown again. He was left with the blue-flecked sky and the grey houses that stood around the gardens like beasts about a water-pool. The sun (a red disc) peered over their shoulders. He went, with his mother within doors. Instantly on his entrance the house began to rustle and whisper.

II

Mrs. Slater, although an amiable and kind-hearted human being who believed with confident superstition in a God of other people's making, did not, on the whole, welcome her lady friends with much cordiality. It was not, as she often explained, as though she had her own house into which to ask them. Her motto was, "Friendly with All, Familiar with None," and to this she very faithfully held. But in her heart there was reason enough for this caution; there had been days—yes, and nights too—when, during her lamented husband's lifetime, she had "taken a drop," taken it, obviously enough, as a comfort, and a solace when things were going very hard with her, and "'Enery preferrin' 'er to be jolly 'erself to keep 'im company." She had protested, but Fate and Henry had been too strong for her. "She had fallen into the habit!" Then, when No. 21 had come under her care, she had put it all sternly behind her, but one did not know how weak one might be, and a kindly friend might with her persuasion—

Therefore did Mrs. Slater avoid her kindly friends. There was, however, one friend who was not so readily to be avoided; that was Mrs. Carter. Mrs. Carter also was a widow, or rather, to speak the direct truth, had discovered one morning, twenty years ago, that Mr. Carter "was gone"; he had never returned. Those who knew Mrs. Carter intimately said that, on the whole, "things bein' as they was," his departure was not entirely to be wondered at. Mrs. Carter had a temper of her own, and nothing inflamed it so much as a drop of whisky, and there was nothing in the world she liked so much as "a drop."

To meet her casually, you would judge her nothing less than the most amiable of womankind—a large, stout, jolly woman, with a face like a rose, and a quantity of black hair. At her best, in her fine Sunday clothes, she was a superb figure, and wore round her neck a rope of sham pearls that would have done credit to a sham countess. During the week, however, she slipped, on occasion, into "déshabille," and then she appeared not quite so attractive. No one knew the exact nature of her profession. She did a bit of "char"; she had at one time a little sweetshop, where she sold sweets, the *Police Budget*, and—although this was revealed only to her best friends—indecent photographs. It may be that the police discovered some of the sources of her income; at any rate the sweetshop was suddenly, one morning, abandoned. Her movements in everything were sudden; it was quite suddenly that she took a fancy to Mrs. Slater. She met her at a friend's, and at once, so she told Mrs. Slater, "I liked yer, just as though I'd met yer before. But I'm like that. Sudden or not at all is *my* way, and not a bad way either!"

Mrs. Slater could not be said to be everything that was affectionate in return. She distrusted Mrs. Carter, disliked her brilliant colouring and her fluent experiences, felt shy before her rollicking suggestiveness, and timid at her innuendoes. For a considerable time she held her defences against the insidious attack. Then there came a day when Mrs. Carter burst into reluctant but passionate tears, asserting that Life and Mr. Carter had been, from the beginning, against her; that she had committed, indeed, acts of folly in the past, but only when driven desperately against a wall; that she bore no grudge against any one alive, but loved all humanity; that she was going to do her best to be a better woman, but couldn't really hope to arrive at any satisfactory improvement without Mrs. Slater's assistance; that Mrs. Slater, indeed, had shown her a New Way, a New Light, a New Path.

Mrs. Slater, humble woman, had no illusions as to her own importance in the scheme of things; nothing touched her so surely as an appeal to her strength of character. She received Mrs. Carter with open arms, suggested that they should read the Bible together on Sunday mornings, and go, side by side, to St. Matthew's on Sunday evenings. There was nothing like a study of the "Holy Word" for "defeating the bottle," and there was nothing like "defeating the bottle" for getting back one's strength and firmness of character.

It was along these lines that Mrs. Slater proposed to conduct Mrs. Carter.

Now unfortunately Henry took an instant and truly savage dislike to his mother's new friend. He had been always, of course, "odd" in his feelings about people, but never was he "odder" than he was with Mrs. Carter. "Little lamb," she said, when she saw him for the first time. "I envy you that child, Mrs. Slater, I do indeed. Backwards 'e may be, but 'is being dependent, as you may say, touches the 'eart. Little lamb!"

She tried to embrace him; she offered him sweets. He shuddered at her approach, and his face was instantly grey, like a pool the moment after the sun's setting. Had he been himself able to put into words his sensations, he would have said that the sight of Mrs. Carter assured him, quite definitely, that something horrible would soon occur.

The house upon whose atmosphere he so depended instantly darkened; his Friend was gone, not because he was no longer able to see him (his consciousness of him did not depend at all upon any visual assurance), but because there was now, Henry was perfectly assured, no chance whatever of his suddenly appearing. And, on the other hand, those Others—the one with the taloned claws behind the piano, the one with the black-hooded eyes—were stronger, more threatening, more dominating. But, beyond her influence on the house, Mrs. Carter, in her own physical and actual presence, tortured Henry. When she was in the room, Henry suffered agony. He would creep away were he allowed, and, if that were not possible, then he would retreat into the most distant corner and watch. If he were in the room his eyes never left Mrs. Carter for a moment, and it was this brooding gaze more than his disapproval that irritated her. "You never can tell with poor little dears when they're 'queer' what fancies they'll take. Why, he quite seems to dislike me, Mrs. Slater!"

Mrs. Slater could venture no denial; indeed, Henry's attitude aroused once again in her mind her earlier suspicions. She had all the reverence of her class for her son's "oddness." He knew more than ordinary mortal folk, and could see farther; he saw beyond Mrs. Carter's red cheeks and shining black hair, and the fact that he was, as a rule, tractable to cheerful kindness, made his rejection the more remarkable. But it might, nevertheless, be that the black things in Mrs. Carter's past were the marks impressed upon Henry's sensitive intelligence; and that he had not, as yet, perceived the new Mrs. Carter growing in grace now day by day.

"'E'll get over 'is fancy, bless 'is 'eart." Mrs. Slater pursued then her work of redemption.

III

On a certain evening in November, Mrs. Carter, coming in to see her friend, invited sympathy for a very bad cold.

"Drippin' and runnin' at the nose I've been all day, my dear. Awake all night I was with it, and 'tain't often that I've one, but when I do it's somethin' cruel." It seemed to be better this evening, Mrs. Slater thought, but when she congratulated her friend on this, Mrs. Carter, shaking her head, remarked that it had left the nose and travelled into the throat and ears. "Once it's earache, and I'm done," she said. Horrible pictures she drew of this earache, and it presently became clear that Mrs. Carter was in perfect terror of a night made sleepless with pain. Once, it seemed, had Mrs. Carter tried to commit suicide by hanging herself to a nail in a door, so maddening had the torture been. Luckily (Mrs. Carter thanked Heaven) the nail had been dragged from the door by her weight—"not that I was anything very 'eavy, you understand." Finally, it appeared that only one thing in the world could be relied upon to stay the fiend.

Mrs. Carter produced from her pocket a bottle of whisky.

Upon that it followed that, since her reformation, Mrs. Carter had come to loathe the very smell of whisky, and as for the taste of it! But rather than be driven by flaming agony down the long stony passages of a sleepless night—anything.

It was here, of course, that Mrs. Slater should have protested, but, in her heart, she was afraid of her friend, and afraid of herself. Mrs. Carter's company had, of late, been pleasant to her. She had been strengthened in her own resolves towards a fine life by the sight of Mrs. Carter's struggle in that direction, and that good woman's genial amiability (when it was so obvious from her appearance that she could be far otherwise) flattered Mrs. Slater's sense of power. No, she could not now bear to let Mrs. Carter go.

She said, therefore, nothing to her friend about the whisky, and on that evening Mrs. Carter did take the "veriest sip." But the cold continued—it continued in a marvellous and terrible manner. It seemed "to 'ave taken right 'old of 'er system."

After a few evenings it was part of the ceremonies that the bottle should be produced; the kettle was boiling happily on the fire, there was lemon, there was a lump of sugar.... On a certain wet and depressing evening Mrs. Slater herself had a glass "just to see that she didn't get a cold like Mrs. Carter's."

IV

Henry's bed-time was somewhere between the hours of eight
and nine, but his mother did not care to leave Mrs. Carter
(dear friend, though she was) quite alone downstairs with the
bottom half of the house unguarded (although, of course, the
doors were locked), therefore, Mrs. Carter came upstairs with
her friend to see the little fellow put to bed; "and a hangel he
looks, if ever I see one," declared the lady enthusiastically.

When the two were gone and the house was still, Henry would
sit up in bed and listen; then, moving quietly, he would creep
out and listen again.

There, in the passage, it seemed to him that he could hear the
whole house talking—first one sound and then another would
come, the wheeze of some straining floor, the creak of some
whispering board, the shudder of a door. "Look out! Look out!
Look out!" and then, above that murmur, some louder voice:
"Watch! there's danger in the place!" Then, shivering with cold
and his sense of evil, he would creep down into a lower passage
and stand listening again; now the voices of the house were
deafening, rising on every side of him, like the running of little
streams suddenly heard on the turning of the corner of a hill.
The dim light shrouded with fantasy the walls; along the wide
passage and cabinets, high china jars, the hollow scoop of the
window at the far-distant end, were all alive and moving. And,
in strange contradiction to the moving voices within the
house, came the blurred echo of the London life, whirring,
buzzing, like a cloud of gnats at the window-pane. "Look out!
Look out! Look out!" the house cried, and Henry, with
chattering teeth, was on guard.

There came an evening when standing thus, shivering in his
little shirt, he was aware that the terror, so long anticipated,
was upon him. It seemed to him, on this evening, that the
house was suddenly still; it was as though all the sounds, as of
running water, that passed up and down the rooms and
passages, were, in a flashing second, frozen. The house was

holding its breath.

He had to wait for a breathless, agonising interval before he heard the next sound, very faint and stifled breathing coming up to him out of the darkness in little uncertain gusts. He heard the breathings pause, then recommence again in quicker and louder succession. Henry, stirred simply, perhaps, by the terror of his anticipation, moved back into the darker shadows in the nook of the cabinet, and stayed there with his shirt pressed against his little trembling knees.

Then followed, after a long time, a half yellow circle of light that touched the top steps of the stairs and a square of the wall; behind the light was the stealthy figure of Mrs. Carter. She stood there for a moment, one hand with a candle raised, the other pressed against her breast; from one finger of this hand a bunch of heavy keys dangled. She stood there, with her wide, staring eyes, like glass in the candle-light, staring about her, her red cheeks rising and falling with her agitation, her body seeming enormous, her shadow on the wall huge in the flickering light. At the sight of his enemy Henry's terror was so frantic that his hands beat with little spasmodic movements against the wall.

He did not *see* Mrs. Carter at all, but he saw rather the movement through the air and darkness of the house of something that would bring down upon him the full naked force of the Terror that he had all his life anticipated. He had always known that the awful hour would arrive when the Terror would grip him; again and again he had seen its eyes, felt its breath, heard its movements, and these movements had been forewarnings of some future day. That day had arrived.

There was only one thing that he could do; his Friend alone in all the world could help him. With his soul dizzy and faint from fear, he prayed for his Friend; had he been less frightened he would have screamed aloud for him to come and help him.

The boy's breath came hot into his throat and stuck there, and his heart beat like a high, unresting hammer.

Mrs. Carter, with the candle raised to throw light in front of her, moved forward very cautiously and softly. She passed down the passage, and then paused very near to the boy. She looked at the keys, and stole like some heavy, stealthy animal to the door of the long drawing-room. He watched her as she tried one key after another, making little dissatisfied noises as they refused to fit; then at last one turned the lock and she pushed back the door.

It was certainly impossible for him, in the dim world of his mind, to realise what it was that she intended to do, but he knew, through some strange channel of knowledge, that his mother was concerned in this, and that something more than the immediate peril of himself was involved. He had also, lost in the dim mazes of his mind, a consciousness that there *were* treasures in the house, and that his mother was placed there to guard them, and even that he himself shared her duty.

It did not come to him that Mrs. Carter was in pursuit of these treasures, but he *did* realise that her presence there amongst them brought peril to his mother. Moved then by some desperate urgency which had at its heart his sense that to be left alone in the black passage was worse than the actual lighted vision of his Terror, he crept with trembling knees across the passage and through the door.

Inside the room he saw that she had laid the candle upon the piano, and was bending over a drawer, trying again to fit a key. He stood in the doorway, a tiny figure, very, very cold, all his soul in his silent appeal for some help. His Friend *must* come. He was somewhere there in the house. "Come! Help me!" The candle suddenly flared into a finger of light that flung the room into vision. Mrs. Carter, startled, raised herself, and at that same moment Henry gave a cry, a weak little trembling sound.

She turned and saw the boy; as their eyes met he felt the

Terror rushing upon him. He flung a last desperate appeal for help, staring at her as though his eyes would never let her go, and she, finding him so unexpectedly, could only gape. In their silent gaze at one another, in the glassy stare of Mrs. Carter and the trembling, flickering one of Henry there was more than any ordinary challenge could have conveyed. Mrs. Carter must have felt at the first immediate confrontation of the strange little figure that her feet were on the very edge of some most desperate precipice. The long room and the passages beyond must have quivered. At that very first moment, with some stir, some hinted approach, Henry called, with the desperate summoning of all his ghostly world, upon his gods. They came....

In her eyes he saw suddenly something else than vague terror. He saw recognition. He felt himself a rushing, heartening comfort; he knew that his Friend had somehow come, that he was no longer alone.

But Mrs. Carter's eyes were staring beyond him, over him, into the black passage. Her eyes seemed to grow as though the terror in them was pushing them out beyond their lids; her breath, came in sharp, tearing gasps. The keys with a clang dropped from her hand.

"Oh, God! Oh, God!" she whispered. He did not turn his head to grasp what it was that she saw in the passage. The terror had been transferred from himself to her.

The colour in her cheeks went out, leaving her as though her face were suddenly shadowed by some overhanging shape.

Her eyes never moved nor faltered from the dark into whose heart she gazed. Then, there was a strangled, gasping cry, and she sank down, first onto her knees, then in a white faint, her eyes still staring, lay huddled on the floor.

Henry felt his Friend's hand on his shoulder.

Meanwhile, down in the kitchen, the fire had sunk into grey ashes, and Mrs. Slater was lying back in her chair, her head back, snoring thickly; an empty glass had tumbled across the table, and a few drops from it had dribbled over on to the tablecloth.

CHAPTER VII

BARBARA FLINT

I

Barbara Flint was a little girl, aged seven, who lived with her parents at No. 36 March Square. Her brother and sister, Master Anthony and Miss Misabel Flint, were years and years older, so you must understand that she led rather a solitary life. She was a child with very pale flaxen hair, very pale blue eyes, very pale cheeks—she looked like a china doll who had been left by a careless mistress out in the rain. She was a very sensitive child, cried at the least provocation, very affectionate, too, and ready to imagine that people didn't like her.

Mr. Flint was a stout, elderly gentleman, whose favourite pursuit was to read the newspapers in his club, and to inveigh against the Liberals. He was pale and pasty, and suffered from indigestion. Mrs. Flint was tall, thin and severe, and a great helper at St. Matthew's, the church round the corner. She gave up all her time to church work and the care of the poor, and it wasn't her fault that the poor hated her. Between the Scylla of politics and the Charybdis of religion there was very little left for poor Barbara; she faded away under the care of an elderly governess who suffered from a perfect cascade of ill-fated love affairs; it seemed that gentlemen were always "playing with her feelings." But in all probability a too vivid imagination led her astray in this matter; at any rate, she cried so often during Barbara's lessons that the title of the lesson-book, "Reading

Hugh Walpole

without Tears," was sadly belied. It might be expected that, under these unfavourable circumstances, Barbara was growing into a depressed and melancholy childhood.

Barbara, happily, was saved by her imagination. Surely nothing quite like Barbara's imagination had ever been seen before, because it came to her, outside inheritance, outside environment, outside observation. She had it altogether, in spite of Flints past and present. But, perhaps, not altogether in spite of March Square. It would be difficult to say how deeply the fountain, the almond tree, the green, flat shining grass had stung her intuition; but stung it only, not created it—the thing was there from the beginning of all time. She talked, at first to nurses, servants, her mother, about the things that she knew; about her Friend who often came to see her, who was there so many times—there in the room with her when they couldn't catch a glimpse of him: about the days and nights when she was away anywhere, up in the sky, out on the air, deep in the sea, about all the other experiences that she remembered but was now rapidly losing consciousness of. She talked, at first easily, naturally, and inviting, as it were, return confidences. Then, quite suddenly, she realised that she simply wasn't believed, that she was considered a wicked little girl "for making things up so," that there was no hope at all for her unless she abandoned her "lying ways."

The shock of this discovery flung her straight back upon herself; if they refused to believe these things, then there was nothing to be done. But for herself their incredulity should not stop her. She became a very quiet little girl—what her nurse called "brooding." This incredulity of theirs drove them all instantly into a hostile camp, and the affection that she had been longing to lavish upon them must now be reserved for other, and, she could not help feeling, wiser persons. This division of herself from the immediate world hurt her very much. From a very early age, indeed, we need reassurance as to the necessity for our existence. Barbara simply did not seem to be wanted.

But still worse: now that her belief in certain things had been challenged, she herself began to question them. Was it true, possibly, when a flaming sunset struck a sword across the Square and caught the fountain, slashing it into a million glittering fragments, that that was all that occurred? Such a thing had been for Barbara simply a door into her earlier world. See the fountain—well, you have been tested; you are still simple enough to go back into the real world. But was Barbara simple enough? She was seven; it is just about then that we begin, under the guard of nurses carefully chosen for us by our parents, to drop our simplicity. It must, of course, be so, or the world would be all dreamers, and then there would be no commerce.

Barbara knew nothing of commerce, but she did know that she was unhappy, that her dolls gave her no happiness, and that her Friend did not come now so often to see her. She was, I am afraid, in character a "Hopper." She must be affectionate, she must demand affection of others, and will they not give it her, then must they simulate it. The tragedy of it all was perhaps, that Barbara had not herself that coloured vitality in her that would prepare other people to be fond of her. The world is divided between those who place affection about, now here, now there, and those whose souls lie, like drawers, unawares, but ready for the affection to be laid there.

Barbara could not "place" it about; she had neither optimism nor a sense of humour sufficient. But she wanted it—wanted it terribly. If she were not to be allowed to indulge her imagination, then must she, all the more, love some one with fervour: the two things were interdependent. She surveyed her world with an eye to this possible loving. There was her governess, who had been with her for a year now, tearful, bony, using Barbara as a means and never as an end. Barbara did not love her—how could she? Moreover, there were other physical things: the lean, shining marble of Miss Letts's long fingers, the dry thinness of her hair, the way that the tip of her nose would be suddenly red, and then, like a blown-out candle, dull white again. Fingers and noses are not the only agents in the human affections, but they have most certainly something to do with them. Moreover, Miss Letts was too busily engaged with the survey of her relations, with now this gentleman, now that, to pay much attention to Barbara. She dismissed her as "a queer little thing." There were in Miss Letts's world "queer things" and "things not queer." The division was patent to anybody.

Barbara's father and mother were also surveyed. Here Barbara was baffled by the determination on the part of both of them that she should talk, should think, should dream about all the things concerning which she could not talk, think nor dream. "How to grow up into a nice little girl," "How to pray to God," "How never to tell lies," "How to keep one's clothes clean,"—these things did not interest Barbara in the least; but had she been given love with them she might have paid some attention. But a too rigidly defined politics, a too rigidly defined religion find love a poor, loose, sentimental thing— very rightly so, perhaps. Mrs. Flint was afraid that Barbara was a "silly little girl."

"I hope, Miss Letts, that she no longer talks about her silly fancies."

"She has said nothing to me in that respect for a considerable period, Mrs. Flint."

"All very young children have fancies, but such things are dangerous when they grow older."

"I agree with you."

Nevertheless the fountain continued to flash in the sun, and births, deaths, weddings, love and hate continued to play their part in March Square.

II

Barbara, groping about in the desolation of having no one to grope with her, discovered that her Friend came now less frequently to see her. She was even beginning to wonder whether he had ever really come at all. She had perhaps imagined him just as on occasion she would imagine her doll, Jane, the Queen of England, or her afternoon tea the most wonderful meal, with sausages, blackberry jam and chocolates. Young though, she was, she was able to realise that this imagination of hers was *capable de tout*, and that every one older than herself said that it was wicked; therefore was her Friend, perhaps, wicked also.

And yet, if the dark curtains that veiled the nursery windows at night, if the glimmering shape of the picture-frames, if the square black sides of the dolls' house were real, real also was the figure of her Friend, real his arousal in her of all the memories of the old days before she was Barbara Flint at all—real, too, his love, his care, his protection; as real, yes, as Miss Letts's bony figure. It was all very puzzling. But he did not come now as in the old days.

Barbara played very often in the gardens in the middle of the Square, but because she was a timid little girl she did not make many friends. She knew many of the other children who played there, and sometimes she shared in their games; but her sensitive feelings were so easily hurt, she frequently retired in tears. Every day on going into the garden she looked about her, hoping that she would find before she left it again some one whom it would be possible to worship. She tried on several occasions to erect altars, but our English temperament is against public display, and she was misunderstood.

Then, quite suddenly, as though she had sprung out of the fountain, Mary Adams was there. Mary Adams was aged nine, and her difference from Barbara Flint was that, whereas Barbara craved for affection, she craved for attention: the two demands can be easily confused. Mary Adams was the only child of an aged philosopher, Mr. Adams, who, contrary to all that philosophy teaches, had married a young wife. The young wife, pleased that Mary was so unlike her father, made much of her, and Mary was delighted to be made much of. She was a little girl with flaxen hair, blue eyes, and a fine pink-and-white colouring. In a few years' time she will be so sure of the attention that her appearance is winning for her that she will make no effort to secure adherents, but just now she is not sufficiently confident—she must take trouble. She took trouble with Barbara.

Sitting neatly upon a seat, Mary watched rude little boys throw sidelong glances in her direction. Her long black legs were quivering with the perception of their interest, even though her eyes were haughtily indifferent. It was then that Barbara, with Miss Letts, an absent-minded companion, came and sat by her side. Barbara and Mary had met at a party—not quite on equal terms, because nine to seven is as sixty to thirty—but they had played hide-and-seek together, and had, by chance, hidden in the same cupboard.

The little boys had moved away, and Mary Adams's legs dropped, suddenly, their tension.

"I'm going to a party to-night," Mary said, with a studied indifference.

Miss Letts knew of Mary's parents, and that, socially, they were "all right"—a little more "all right," were we to be honest, than Mr. and Mrs. Flint. She said, therefore:

"Are you, dear? That will be nice for you."

Instantly Barbara was trembling with excitement. She knew that the remark had been made to her and not at all to Miss Letts. Barbara entered once again, and instantly, upon the field of the passions. Here she was fated by her temperament to be in all cases a miserable victim, because panic, whether she were accepted or rejected by the object of her devotion, reduced her to incoherent foolishness; she could only be foolish now, and, although her heart beat like a leaping animal inside her, allowed Miss Letts to carry on the conversation.

But Miss Letts's wandering eye hurt Mary's pride. She was not really interested in her, and once Mary had come to that conclusion about any one, complete, utter oblivion enveloped them. She perceived, however, Barbara's agitation, and at that, flattered and appeased, she was amiable again. There followed between the two a strangled and disconnected conversation.

Mary began:

"I've got four dolls at home."

"Have you?" breathlessly from Barbara. By such slow accuracies as these are we conveyed, all our poor mortal days, from realism to romance, and with a shocking precipitance are we afterwards flung back, out of romance into realism, our natural home, again.

"Yes—four dolls I have. My mother will give me another if I ask her. Would your mother?"

"Yes," said Barbara, untruthfully.

"That's my governess, Miss Marsh, there, with the green hat, that is. I've had her two months."

"Yes," said Barbara, gazing with adoring eyes.

"She's going away next week. There's another coming. I can do sums, can you?"

"Yes," again from Barbara.

"I can do up to twice-sixty-three. I'm nine. Miss Marsh says I'm clever."

"I'm seven," said Barbara.

"I could read when I was seven—long, long words. Can you read?"

At this moment there arrived the green-hatted Miss Marsh, a plump, optimistic person, to whom Miss Letts was gloomily patronising. Miss Letts always distrusted stoutness in another; it looked like deliberate insult. Mary Adams was conveyed away; Barbara was bereft of her glory.

But, rather, on that instant that Mary Adams vanished did she become glorified. Barbara had been too absurdly agitated to transform on to the mirror of her brain Mary's appearance. In all the dim-coloured splendour of flame and mist was Mary now enwrapped, with every step that Barbara took towards her home did the splendour grow.

III

Then followed an invitation to tea from Mary's mother. Barbara, preparing for the event, suffered her hair to be brushed, choked with strange half-sweet, half-terrible suffocation that comes from anticipated glories: half-sweet because things will, at their worst, be wonderful; half-terrible because we know that they will not be so good as we hope.

Barbara, washed paler than ever, in a white frock with pink bows, was conducted by Miss Letts. She choked with terror in the strange hall, where she was received with great splendour by Mary. The schoolroom was large and fine and bright, finer far than Barbara's room, swamped by the waters of religion and politics. Barbara could only gulp and gulp, and feel still at her throat that half-sweet, half-terrible suffocation. Within her little body her heart, so huge and violent, was pounding.

"A very nice room indeed," said Miss Letts, more friendly now to the optimist because she was leaving in a day or two, and could not, therefore, at the moment be considered a success. Her failure balanced her plumpness.

Here, at any rate, was the beginning of a great friendship between Barbara Flint and Mary Adams. The character of Mary Adams was admittedly a difficult one to explore; her mother, a cloud of nurses and a company of governesses had been baffled completely by its dark caverns and recesses. One clue, beyond question, was selfishness; but this quality, by the very obviousness of it, may tempt us to believe that that is all. It may account, when we are displeased, for so much. It accounted for a great deal with Mary—but not all. She had, I believe, a quite genuine affection for Barbara, nothing very disturbing, that could rival the question as to whether she would receive a second helping of pudding or no, or whether she looked better in blue or pink. Nevertheless, the affection was there. During several months she considered Barbara more than she had ever considered any one in her life before. At that first tea party she was aware, perhaps, that Barbara's proffered devotion was for complete and absolute self-sacrifice, something that her vanity would not often find to feed it. There was, too, no question of comparison between them.

Even when Barbara grew to be nine she would be a poor thing beside the lusty self-confidence of Mary Adams—and this was quite as it should be. All that Barbara wanted was some one upon whom she might pour her devotion, and one of the things that Mary wanted was some one who would spend it upon her. But there stirred, nevertheless, some breath of emotion across that stagnant little pool, Mary's heart. She was moved, perhaps, by pity for Barbara's amazing simplicities, moved also by curiosity as to how far Barbara's devotion to her would go, moved even by some sense of distrust of her own self-satisfaction. She did, indeed, admire any one who could realise, as completely as did Barbara, the greatness of Mary Adams.

It may seem strange to us, and almost terrible, that a small child of seven can feel anything as devastating as this passion of

Barbara. But Barbara was made to be swept by storms stronger than she could control, and Mary Adams was the first storm of her life. They spent now a great deal of their time together. Mrs. Adams, who was beginning to find Mary more than she could control, hailed the gentle Barbara with joy; she welcomed also perhaps a certain note of rather haughty protection which Mary seemed to be developing.

During the hours when Barbara was alone she thought of the many things that she would say to her friend when they met, and then at the meeting could say nothing. Mary talked or she did not talk according to her mood, but she soon made it very plain that there was only one way of looking at everything inside and outside the earth, and that was Mary's way. Barbara had no affection, but a certain blind terror for God. It was precisely as though some one were standing with a hammer behind a tree, and were waiting to hit you on the back of your head at the first opportunity. But God was not, on the whole, of much importance; her Friend was the great problem, and before many days were passed Mary was told all about him.

"He used to come often and often. He'd be there just where you wanted him—when the light was out or anything. And he *was* nice." Barbara sighed.

Mary stared at her, seeming in the first full sweep of confidence, to be almost alarmed.

"You don't mean—?" She stopped, then cried, "Why, you silly, you believe in ghosts!"

"No, I don't," said Barbara, not far from tears.

"Yes, you do."

"No, I don't."

"Of course you do, you silly."

"No, I don't. He—he's real."

"Well," Mary said, with a final toss of the head, "if you go seeing ghosts like that you can't have me for your friend, Barbara Flint—you can choose, that's all."

Barbara was aghast. Such a catastrophe had never been contemplated. Lose Mary? Sooner life itself. She resolved, sorrowfully, to say no more about her Friend. But here occurred a strange thing. It was as though Mary felt that over this one matter Barbara had eluded her; she returned to it again and again, always with contemptuous but inquisitive allusion.

"Did he come last night, Barbara?"

"No."

"P'r'aps he did, only you were asleep."

"No, he didn't."

"You don't believe he'll come ever any more, do you? Now that I've said he isn't there really?"

"Yes, I do."

"Very well, then, I won't see you to-morrow—not at all—not all day—I won't."

These crises tore Barbara's spirit. Seven is not an age that can reason with life's difficulties, and Barbara had, in this business, no reasoning powers at all. She would die for Mary; she could not deny her Friend. What was she to do? And yet—just at this moment when, of all others, it was important that he should come to her and confirm his reality—he made no sign. Not only did he make no sign, but he seemed to withdraw, silently and surely, all his supports. Barbara discovered that the company of Mary Adams did in very truth make everything that was not sure and certain absurd and impossible. There was visible no longer, as there had been before, that country wherein anything was possible, where wonderful things had occurred and where wonderful things would surely occur again.

"You're pretending," said Mary Adams sharply when Barbara ventured some possibly extravagant version of some ordinary occurrence, or suggested that events, rich and wonderful, had occurred during the night. "Nonsense," said Mary sharply.

She said "nonsense" as though it were the very foundation of her creed of life—as, indeed, to the end of her days, it was. What, then, was Barbara to do? Her friend would not come, although passionately she begged and begged and begged that he would. Mary Adams was there every day, sharp, and shining, and resolved, demanding the whole of Barbara Flint, body and soul—nothing was to be kept from her, nothing. What was Barbara Flint to do?

She denied her Friend, denied that earlier world, denied her dreams and her hopes. She cried a good deal, was very lonely in the dark. Mary Adams, as was her way, having won her victory, passed on to win another.

IV

Mary began, now, to find Barbara rather tiresome. Having forced her to renounce her gods, she now despised her for so easy a renunciation. Every day did she force Barbara through her act of denial, and the Inquisition of Spain held, in all its records, nothing more cruel.

"Did he come last night?"

"No."

"He'll never come again, will he?"

"No."

"Wasn't it silly of you to make up stories like that?"

"Oh, Mary—yes."

"There aren't ghosts, nor fairies, nor giants, nor wizards, nor Santa Claus?"

"No; but, Mary, p'r'aps—"

"No; there aren't. Say there aren't."

"There isn't."

Poor Barbara, even as she concluded this ceremony, clutching her doll close to her to give her comfort, could not refrain from a hurried glance over her shoulder. He *might* be— But upon Mary this all began soon enough to pall. She liked some opposition. She liked to defeat people and trample on them and then be gracious. Barbara was a poor little thing. Moreover, Barbara's standard of morality and righteousness annoyed her. Barbara seemed to have no idea that there was anything in this confused world of ours except wrong and right. No dialectician, argue he ever so stoutly, could have persuaded Barbara that there was such a colour in the world's paint-box as grey. "It's bad to tell lies. It's bad to steal. It's bad to put your tongue out. It's good to be kind to poor people. It's good to say 'No' when you want more pudding but mustn't have it." Barbara was no prig. She did not care the least little thing about these things, nor did she ever mention them, but let a question of conduct arise, then was Barbara's way plain and clear. She did not always take it, but there it was. With Mary, how very different! She had, I am afraid, no sense of right and wrong at all, but only a coolly ironical perception of the things that her elders disliked and permitted. Very foolish and absurd, these elders. We have always before our eyes some generation that provokes our irony, the one before us, the one behind us, our own perhaps; for Mary

Adams it would always be any generation that was not her own. Her business in life was to avoid unpleasantness, to extract the honey from every flower, but above all to be admired, praised, preferred.

At first with her pleasure at Barbara's adoration she had found, within herself, a truly alarming desire to be "good." It might, after all, be rather amusing to be, in strict reality, all the fine things that Barbara considered her. She endeavoured for a week or two to adjust herself to this point of view, to consider, however slightly, whether it were right or wrong to do something that she particularly wished to do.

But she found it very tiresome. The effort spoilt her temper, and no one seemed to notice any change. She might as well be bad as good were there no one present to perceive the difference. She gave it up, and, from that moment found that she suffered Barbara less gladly than before. Meanwhile, in Barbara also strange forces had been at work. She found that her imagination (making up stories) simply, in spite of all the Mary Adamses in the world, refused to stop. Still would the almond tree and the fountain, the gold dust on the roofs of the houses when the sun was setting, the racing hurry of rain drops down the window-pane, the funny old woman with the red shawl who brought plants round in a wheelbarrow, start her story telling.

Still could she not hold herself from fancying, at times, that her doll Jane was a queen, and that Miss Letts could make "spells" by the mere crook of her bony fingers. Worst of all, still she must think of her Friend, tell herself with an ache that he would never come back again, feel, sometimes, that she would give up Mary and all the rest of the world if he would only be beside her bed, as he used to be, talking to her, holding her hand. During these days, had there been any one to observe her, she was a pathetic little figure, with her thin legs like black sticks, her saucer eyes that so readily filled with tears, her eager, half-apprehensive expression, the passionate clutch of the doll to her heart, and it is, after all, a painful business, this adoration—no human soul can live up to the heights of it, and, what is more, no human soul ought to.

As Mary grew tired of Barbara she allowed to slip from her many of the virtuous graces that had hitherto, for Barbara's benefit, adorned her. She lost her temper, was cruel simply for the pleasure that Barbara's ill-restrained agitation yielded her, but, even beyond this, squandered recklessly her reputation for virtue. Twice, before Barbara's very eyes, she told lies, and told them, too, with a real mastery of the craft—long practice and a natural disposition had brought her very near perfection. Barbara, her heart beating wildly, refused to understand; Mary could not be so. She held Jane to her breast more tightly than before. And the denials continued; twice a day now they were extorted from her—with every denial the ghost of her Friend stole more deeply into the mist. He was gone; he was gone; and what was left?

Very soon, and with unexpected suddenness, the crisis came.

V

Upon a day Barbara accompanied her mother to tea with Mrs. Adams. The ladies remained downstairs in the dull splendour of the drawing-room; Mary and Barbara were delivered to Miss Fortescue, the most recent guardian of Mary's life and prospects.

"She's simply awful. You needn't mind a word she says," Mary instructed her friend, and prepared then to behave accordingly. They had tea, and Mary did as she pleased. Miss Fortescue protested, scolded, was weak when she should have been strong, and said often, "Now, Mary, there's a dear."

Barbara, the faint colour coming and going in her cheeks, watched. She watched Mary now with quite a fresh intention. She had begun her voyage of discovery: what was in Mary's head, *what* would she do next? What Mary did next was to propose, after tea, that they should travel through other parts of the house.

"We'll be back in a moment," Mary flung over her head to Miss Fortescue. They proceeded then through passages, peering into dark rooms, looking behind curtains, Barbara following behind her friend, who seemed to be moved by a rather aimless intention of finding something to do that she shouldn't. They finally arrived at Mrs. Adams's private and particular sitting-room, a place that may be said, in the main, to stand as a protest against the rule of the ancient philosopher, being all pink and flimsy and fragile with precious vases and two post-impressionist pictures (a green apple tree one, the other a brown woman), and lace cushions and blue bowls with rose leaves in them. Barbara had never been into this room before, nor had she ever in all her seven years seen anything so lovely.

"Mother says I'm never to come in here," announced Mary. "But I do—lots. Isn't it pretty?"

"P'r'aps we oughtn't—" began Barbara.

"Oh, yes, we ought," answered Mary scornfully. "Always you and your 'oughtn't.'"

She turned, and her shoulders brushed a low bracket that was close to the door. A large Nankin vase was at her feet, scattered into a thousand pieces. Even Mary's proud indifference was stirred by this catastrophe, and she was down on her knees in an instant, trying to pick up the pieces. Barbara stared, her eyes wide with horror.

"Oh, Mary," she gasped.

"You might help instead of just standing there!"

Then the door opened and, like the avenging gods from Olympus, in came the two ladies, eagerly, with smiles.

"Now I must just show you," began Mrs. Adams. Then the catastrophe was discovered—a moment's silence, then a cry from the poor lady: "Oh, my vase! It was priceless!" (It was not, but no matter.)

About Barbara the air clung so thick with catastrophe that it was from a very long way indeed that she heard Mary's voice:

"Barbara didn't mean—"

"Did you do this, Barbara?" her mother turned round upon her.

"You know, Mary, I've told you a thousand times that you're not to come in here!" this from Mrs. Adams, who was obviously very angry indeed.

Mary was on her feet now and, as she looked across at Barbara, there was in her glance a strange look, ironical, amused, inquisitive, even affectionate. "Well, mother, I knew we mustn't. But Barbara wanted to *look* so I said we'd just *peep*, but that we weren't to touch anything, and then Barbara couldn't help it, really; her shoulder just brushed the shelf—" and still as she looked there was in her eyes that strange irony: "Well, now you see me as I am—I'm bored by all this pretending. It's gone on long enough. Are you going to give me away?"

But Barbara could do nothing. Her whole world was there, like the Nankin vase, smashed about her feet, as it never, never would be again.

"So you did this, Barbara?" Mrs. Flint said.

"Yes," said Barbara. Then she began to cry.

VI

At home she was sent to bed. Her mother read her a chapter of the Gospel according to St. Matthew, and then left her; she lay there, sick with crying, her eyes stiff and red, wondering how she would ever get through the weeks and weeks of life that remained to her. She thought: "I'll never love any one again. Mary took my Friend away—and then she wasn't there herself. There isn't anybody."

Then it suddenly occurred to her that she need never be put through the agony of her denials again, that she could believe what she liked, make up stories.

Her Friend would, of course, never come to see her any more, but at least now she would be able to think about him. She would be allowed to remember. Her brain was drowsy, her eyes half closed. Through the humming air something was coming; the dark curtains were parted, the light of the late afternoon sun was faint yellow upon the opposite wall—there was a little breeze. Drowsily, drowsily, her drooping eyes felt the light, the stir of the air, the sense that some one was in the room.

She looked up; she gave a cry! He had come back! He had come back after all!

CHAPTER VIII

SARAH TREFUSIS

I

Sarah Trefusis lived, with her mother, in the smallest house in March Square, a really tiny house, like a box, squeezed breathlessly between two fat buildings, but looking, with its white paint and green doors, smarter than either of them. Lady Charlotte Trefusis, Sarah's mother, was elegant, penniless and a widow; Captain B. Trefusis, her husband, had led the merriest of lives until a game of polo carried him reluctantly from a delightful world and forced Lady Charlotte to consider the problem of having a good time alone on nothing at all. But it may be said that, on the whole, she succeeded. She was the best-dressed widow in London, and went everywhere, but the little house in March Square was the scene of a most strenuous campaign, every day presenting its defeat or victory, and every minute of the day threatening overwhelming disaster if something were not done immediately. Lady Charlotte had the smallest feet and hands outside China, a pile of golden hair above the face of a pink-and-white doll. Staring from this face, however, were two of the loveliest, most unscrupulous of eyes, and those eyes did more for Lady Charlotte's precarious income than any other of her resources. She wore her expensive clothes quite beautifully, and gave lovely little lunches and dinners; no really merry house-party was complete without her.

Sarah was her only child, and, although at the time of which I am writing she was not yet nine years of age, there was no one in London better suited to the adventurous and perilous existence that Fate had selected for her. Sarah was black as ink—that is, she had coal black hair, coal black eyes, and wonderful black eyelashes. Her eyelashes were her only beautiful feature, but she was, nevertheless, a most remarkable looking child. "If ever a child's possessed of the devil, my dear Charlotte," said Captain James Trent to her mother, "it's your precious daughter—she *is* the devil, I believe."

"Well, she needs to be," said her mother, "considering the life that's in store for her. We're very good friends, she and I, thank you."

They were. They understood one another to perfection. Lady Charlotte was as hard as nails, and Sarah was harder. Sarah had never been known to cry. She had bitten the fingers of one of her nurses through to the bone, and had stuck a needle into the cheek of another whilst she slept, and had watched, with a curious abstracted gaze, the punishment dealt out to her, as though it had nothing to do with her at all. She never lost her temper, and one of the most terrible things about her was her absolute calm. She was utterly fearless, went to the dentist without a tremor, and, at the age of six, fell downstairs, broke her leg, and so lay until help arrived without a cry. She bullied and hurt anything or anybody that came her way, but carried out her plans always with the same deliberate abstraction as though she were obeying somebody's orders. She never nourished revenge or resentment, and it seemed to be her sense of humour (rather than any fierce or hostile feeling) that was tickled when she hurt any one.

She was a child, apparently without imagination, but displayed, at a very early period, a strangely sharpened perception of what her nurse called "the uncanny." She frightened even her mother by the expression that her face often wore of attention to something or somebody outside her companion's perception.

"A broomstick is what she'll be flying away on one of these nights, you mark my word," a nurse declared. "Little devil, she is, neither more nor less. It isn't decent the way she sits on the floor looking right through the wall into the next room, as you might say. Yes, and knows who's coming up the stairs long before she's seen 'em. No place for a decent Christian woman, and so I told her mother this very morning." It was, of course, quite impossible to find a nurse to stay with Sarah, and, when she arrived at the age of seven, nurses were dismissed, and she either looked after herself or was tended by an abandoned French maid of her mother's, who stayed with Lady Charlotte, like a wicked, familiar spirit, for a great number of years on a strange basis of confidante, fellow-plunderer, and sympathetic adventurer. This French maid, whose name was, appropriately enough, Hortense, had a real affection for Sarah "because she was the weeckedest child of 'er age she ever see." There was nothing of which Sarah, from the very earliest age, did not seem aware. Her mother's gentlemen friends she valued according to their status in the house, and, as they "fell off" or "came on," so was her manner indifferent or pleasant. For Hortense, she had a real respect, but even that improper and brazen spirit quailed at times before her cynical and elfish regard. To say of a child that there is something "unearthly" about it is, as a rule, to pay a compliment to ethereal blue and gold. There was nothing ethereal about Sarah, and yet she was unearthly enough. Squatting on the floor, her legs tucked under her, her head thrust forward, her large black eyes staring at the wall, her black hair almost alive in the shining intensity of its colours, she had in her attitude the lithe poise of some animal ready to spring, waiting for its exact opportunity.

When her mother, in a temper, struck her, she would push her hair back from her face with a sharp movement of her hand and then would watch broodingly and cynically for the next move. "You hit me again," she seemed to say, "and you *will* make a fool of yourself."

She was aware, of course, of a thousand influences in the house of which her mother and Hortense had never the slightest conception. From the cosy security of her cradle she had watched the friendly spirit who had accompanied (with hostile irritation) her entrance into this world. His shadow had, for a long period, darkened her nursery, but she repelled, with absolute assurance, His kindly advances.

"I'm not frightened. I don't, in the least, want things made comfortable for me. I can get along very nicely, indeed, without you. You're full of sentiment and gush—things that I detest—and it won't be the least use in the world for you to ask me to be good, and tender, and all the rest of it. I'm not like your other babies."

He must have known, of course, that she was not, but, nevertheless, He stayed "I understand perfectly," He assured her. "But, nevertheless, I don't give you up. You may be, for all you know, more interesting to me than all the others put together. And remember this—every time you do anything at all kind or thoughtful, every time you think of any one or care for them, every time you use your influence for good in any way, my power over you is a little stronger, I shall be a little closer to you, your escape will be a little harder."

"Oh, you needn't flatter yourself," she answered Him. "There's precious little danger of *my* self-sacrifice or love for others. That's not going to be my attitude to life at all. You'd better not waste your time over me."

She had not, she might triumphantly reflect, during these eight years, given Him many chances, and yet He was still there. She hated the thought of His patience, and somewhere deep within herself she dreaded the faint, dim beat of some response that, like a warning bell across a misty sea, cautioned her. "You may think you're safe from Him, but He'll catch you yet."

"He shan't," she replied. "I'm stronger than He is."

II

This must sound, in so prosaic a summary of it, fantastic, but nothing could be said to be fantastic about Sarah. She was, for one thing, quite the least troublesome of children. She could be relied upon, at any time, to find amusement for herself. She was full of resources, but what these resources exactly were it would be difficult to say. She would sit for hours alone, staring in front of her. She never played with toys—she did not draw or read—but she was never dull, and always had the most perfect of appetites. She had never, from the day of her birth, known an hour's illness.

It was, however, in the company of other children that she was most characteristic. The nurses in the Square quite frankly hated her, but most of the mothers had a very real regard for Lady Charlotte's smart little lunches; moreover, it was impossible to detect Sarah's guilt in any positive fashion. It was not enough for the nurses to assure their mistresses that from the instant that the child entered the gardens all the other children were out of temper, rebellious, and finally unmanageable.

"Nonsense, Janet, you imagine things. She seems a very nice little girl."

"Well, ma'am, all I can say is, I won't care to be answerable for Master Ronald's behaviour when she *does* come along, that's all. It's beyond belief the effect she 'as upon 'im."

The strangest thing of all was that Sarah herself liked the company of other children. She went every morning into the gardens (with Hortense) and watched them at their play. She would sit, with her hands folded quietly on her lap, her large black eyes watching, watching, watching. It was odd, indeed, how, instantly, all the children in the garden were aware of her entrance. She, on her part, would appear to regard none of them, and yet would see them all. Perched on her seat she surveyed the gardens always with the same gaze of abstracted interest, watching the clear, decent paths across whose grey background at the period of this episode, the October leaves, golden, flaming, dun, gorgeous and shrivelled, fell through the still air, whirled, and with a little sigh of regret, one might fancy, sank and lay dead. The October colours, a faint haze of smoky mist, the pale blue of the distant sky, the brown moist earth, were gentle, mild, washed with the fading year's regretful tears; the cries of the children, the rhythmic splash of the fountain throbbed behind the colours like some hidden orchestra behind the curtain at the play; the statues in the garden, like fragments of the white bolster clouds that swung so lazily from tree to tree; had no meaning in that misty air beyond the background that they helped to fill. The year, thus idly, with so pleasant a melancholy, was slipping into decay.

Sarah would watch. Then, without a word, she would slip from her seat, and, walking solemnly, rather haughtily, would join some group of children. Day after day the same children came to the gardens, and they all of them knew Sarah by now. Hortense, in her turn also, sitting, stiff and superior, would watch. She would see Sarah's pleasant approach, her smile, her amiability. Very soon, however, there would be trouble—some child would cry out; there would be blows; nurses would run forward, scoldings, protests, captives led away weeping ... and then Sarah would return slowly to her seat, her gaze aloof, cynical, remote. She would carefully explain to Hortense the reason of the uproar. She had done nothing—her conscience was clear. These silly little idiots. She would break into French, culled elaborately from Hortense, would end disdainfully— "mais, voilà,"—very old for her age.

Hortense was vicious, selfish, crude in her pursuit of pleasure, entirely unscrupulous, but, as the days passed, she was, in spite of herself, conscious of some half-acknowledged, half-decided terror of Sarah's possibilities.

The child was eight years old. She was capable of anything; in her remote avoidance of any passion, any regret, any anticipated pleasure, any spontaneity, she was inhuman. Hortense thought that she detected in the chit's mother something of her own fear.

III

There used to come to the gardens a little fat red-faced girl called Mary Kitson, the child of simple and ingenuous parents (her father was a writer of stories of adventure for boys' papers); she was herself simple-minded, lethargic, unadventurous, and happily stupid. Walking one day slowly with Hortense down one of the garden paths, Sarah saw Mary Kitson engaged in talking to two dolls, seated on a bench with them, patting their clothes, very happy, her nurse busy over a novelette.

Sarah stopped.

"I'll sit here," she said, walked across to the bench and sat down. Mary looked up from her dolls, and then, nervously and self-consciously, went back to her play. Sarah stared straight before her.

Hortense amiably endeavoured to draw the nurse into conversation.

"You 'ave 'ere ze fine gardens," she said. "It calls to mind my own Paris. Ah, the gardens in Paris!"

But the nurse had been taught to distrust all foreigners, and her views of Paris were coloured by her reading. She admired Hortense's clothes, but distrusted her advances.

She buried herself even more deeply in the paper. Poor Mary Kitson, alas! found that, in some undefinable manner, the glory had departed from her dolls. Adrian and Emily were, of a sudden, glassy and lumpy abstractions of sawdust and china. Very timidly she raised her large, stupid eyes and regarded Sarah. Sarah returned the glance and smiled. Then she came close to Mary.

"It's better under there," she said, pointing to the shade of a friendly tree.

"May I?" Mary said to her nurse with a frightened gasp.

"Well, now, don't you go far," said the nurse, with a fierce look at Hortense.

"You like where you are?" asked Hortense, smiling more than ever. "You 'ave a good place?" Slowly the nurse yielded. The novelette was laid aside.

Impossible to say what occurred under the tree. Now and again a rustle of wind would send the colours from the trees to short branches loaded with leaves of red gold, shivering through the air; a chequered, blazing canopy covered the ground.

Mary Kitson had, it appeared, very little to say. She sat some way from Sarah, clutching Adrian and Emily tightly to her breast, and always her large, startled eyes were on Sarah's face. She did not move to drive the leaves from her dress; her heart beat very fast, her cheeks were very red.

Sarah talked a little, but not very much. She asked questions about Mary's home and her parents, and Mary answered these interrogations in monosyllabic gasps. It appeared that Mary had a kitten, and that this kitten was a central fact of Mary's existence. The kitten was called Alice.

"Alice is a silly name for a kitten. I shouldn't call a kitten Alice," said Sarah, and Mary started as though in some strange, sinister fashion she were instantly aware that Alice's life and safety were threatened.

From that morning began a strange acquaintance that certainly could not be called a friendship. There could be no question at all that Mary was terrified of Sarah; there could also be no question that Mary was Sarah's obedient slave. The cynical

Hortense, prepared as she was for anything strange and unexpected in Sarah's actions, was, nevertheless, puzzled now.

One afternoon, wet and dismal, the two of them sitting in a little box of a room in the little box of a house, Sarah huddled in a chair, her eyes staring in front of her, Hortense sewing, her white, bony fingers moving sharply like knives, the maid asked a question:

"What do you see—Sar-ah—in that infant?"

"What infant?" asked Sarah, without moving her eyes.

"That Mary with whom now you always are."

"We play games together," said Sarah.

"You do not. You may be playing a game—she does nothing. She is terrified—out of her life."

"She is very silly. It's funny how silly she is. I like her to be frightened."

Mary's nurse told Mary's mother that, in her opinion, Sarah was not a nice child. But Sarah had been invited to tea at the confused, simple abode of the Kitson family, and had behaved perfectly.

"I think you must be wrong, nurse," said Mrs. Kitson. "She seems a very nice little girl. Mary needs companions. It's good for her to be taken out of herself."

Had Mrs. Kitson been of a less confused mind, however, had she had more time for the proper observation of her daughter, she would have noticed her daughter's pale cheeks, her daughter's fits of crying, her daughter's silences. Even as the bird is fascinated by the snake, so was Mary Kitson fascinated by Sarah Trefusis.

"You are torturing that infant," said Hortense, and Sarah smiled.

IV

Mary was by no means the first of Sarah's victim's. There had been many others. Utterly aloof, herself, from all emotions of panic or terror, it had, from the very earliest age, interested her to see those passions at work in others. Cruelty for cruelty's sake had no interest for her at all; to pull the wings from flies, to tie kettles to the tails of agitated puppies, to throw stones at cats, did not, in the least, amuse her. She had once put a cat in the fire, but only because she had seen it play with a terrified mouse. That had affronted her sense of justice. But she was gravely and quite dispassionately interested in the terror of Mary Kitson. In later life a bull fight was to appear to her a tiresome affair, but the domination of one human being over another, absorbing. She had, too, at the very earliest age, that conviction that it was pleasant to combat all sentiment, all appeals to be "good," all soft emotions of pity, anything that could suggest that Right was of more power than Might.

It was as though she said, "You may think that even now you will get me. I tell you I'm a rebel from the beginning; you ll never catch me showing affection or sympathy. If you do you may do your worst."

Beyond all things, her anxiety was that, suddenly, in spite of herself, she would do something "soft," some weak kindness. Her power over Mary Kitson reassured her.

The fascination of this power very soon became to her an overwhelming interest. Playing with Mary Kitson's mind was as absorbing to Sarah, as chess to an older enthusiast; her discoveries promised her a life full of entertainment, if, with her fellow-mortals, she was able, so easily, "to do things," what a time she would always have. She discovered, very soon, that Mary Kitson was, by nature, truthful and obedient, that she had a great fear of God, and that she loved her parents. Here was fine material to work upon. She began by insisting on little lies.

"Say our clocks were all wrong, and you couldn't know what the time was."

"Oh, but—"

"Yes, say it."

"Please, Sarah."

"Say it. Otherwise I'll be punished too. Mind, if you don't say it, I shall know."

There was the horrible threat that effected so much. Mary began soon to believe that Sarah was never absent from her, that she attended her, invisibly, her little dark face peering over Mary's shoulder, and when Mary was in bed at night, the lights out, and only shadows on the walls, Sarah was certainly there, her mocking eyes on Mary's face, her voice whispering things in Mary's ears.

Sarah, Mary very soon discovered, believed in nothing, and knew everything. This horrible combination, naturally, affected Mary, who believed in everything and knew nothing.

"Why should we obey our mothers?" said Sarah. "We're as good as they are."

"Oh, *no*," said Mary, in a voice shocked to a strangled whisper. Nevertheless, she began, a little, to despise her confused parents. There came a day when Mary told a very large lie indeed; she said that she had brushed her teeth when she had not, and she told this lie quite unprompted by Sarah. She was more and more miserable as the days passed.

No one knew exactly the things that the two little girls did when they were alone on an afternoon in Sarah's room. Sarah sent Hortense about her business, and then set herself to the subdual of Mary's mind and character. There would be moments like this, Sarah would turn off the electric light, and the room would be lit only by the dim shining of the evening sky.

"Now, Mary, you go over to that corner—that dark one—and wait there till I tell you to come out. I'll go outside the room, and then you'll see what will happen."

"Oh, no, Sarah, I don't want to."

"Why not, you silly baby?"

"I—I don't want to."

"Well, it will be much worse for you if you don't."

"I want to go home."

"You can after you have done that."

"I want to go home now."

"Go into the corner first."

Sarah would leave the room and Mary would stand with her face to the wall, a trembling prey to a thousand terrors. The light would quiver and shake, steps would tread the floor and cease, there would be a breath in her ears, a wind above her head. She would try to pray, but could remember no words. Sarah would lead her forth, shaking from head to foot.

"You little silly. I was only playing."

Once, and this hurried the climax of the episode, Mary attempted rebellion.

"I want to go home, Sarah."

"Well, you can't. You've got to hear the end of the story first."

"I don't like the story. It's a horrid story. I'm going home."

"You'd better not."

"Yes, I will, and I won't come again, and I won't see you again.
I hate you. I won't. I won't."

Mary, as she very often did, began to cry. Sarah's lips curled
with scorn.

"All right, you can. You'll never see Alice again if you do."

"Alice?"

"Yes, she'll be drowned, and you'll have the toothache, and I'll
come in the middle of the night and wake you."

"I—I don't care. I'm go-going home. I'll t-t-ell m-other."

"Tell her. But look out afterwards, that's all."

Mary remained, but Sarah regarded the rebellion as ominous.
She thought that the time had come to put Mary's submission
really to the test.

V

The climax of the affair was in this manner. Upon an
afternoon when the rain was beating furiously upon the
window-panes and the wind struggling up and down the
chimney, Sarah and Mary played together in Sarah's room; the
play consisted of Mary shutting her eyes and pretending she
was in a dark wood, whilst Sarah was the tiger who might at
any moment spring upon her and devour her, who would, in

Hugh Walpole

any case, pinch her legs with a sudden thrust which would drive all the blood out of Mary's face and make her "as white as the moon."

This game ended, Sarah's black eyes moved about for a fresh diversion; her gaze rested upon Mary, and Mary whispered that she would like to go home.

"Yes. You can,' said Sarah, staring at her, "if you will do something when you get there."

"What?" said Mary, her heart beating like a heavy and jumping hammer.

"There's something I want. You've got to bring it me."

Mary said nothing, only her wide eyes filled with tears.

"There's something in your mother's drawing-room. You know in that little table with the glass top where there are the little gold boxes with the silver crosses and things. There's a ring there—a gold one with a red stone—very pretty. I want it."

Mary drew a long, deep breath. Her fat legs in the tight, black stockings were shaking.

"You can go in when no one sees. The table isn't locked, I know, because I opened it once. You can get and bring it to me to-morrow in the garden."

"Oh," Mary whispered, "that would be stealing."

"Of course it wouldn't. Nobody wants the old ring. No one ever looks at it. It's just for fun."

"No," said Mary, "I mustn't."

"Oh, yes, you must. You'll be very sorry if you don't. Dreadful things will happen. Alice—"

Mary cried softly, choking and spluttering and rubbing her eyes with the back of her hand.

"Well, you'd better go now. I'll be in the garden with Hortense to-morrow. You know, the same place. You'd better have it, that's all. And don't go on crying, or your mother will think I made you. What's there to cry about? No one will eat you."

"It's stealing."

"I dare say it belongs to you, and, anyway, it will when your mother dies, so what *does* it matter? You *are* a baby!"

After Mary's departure Sarah sat for a long while alone in her nursery. She thought to herself: "Mary will be going home now and she'll be snuffling to herself all the way back, and she won't tell the nurse anything, I know that. Now she's in the hall. She's upstairs now, having her things taken off. She's stopped crying, but her eyes and nose are red. She looks very ugly. She's gone to find Alice. She thinks something has happened to her. She begins to cry again when she sees her, and she begins to talk to her about it. Fancy talking to a cat...."

The room was swallowed in darkness, and when Hortense came in and found Sarah sitting alone there, she thought to herself that, in spite of the profits that she secured from her mistress she would find another situation. She did not speak to Sarah, and Sarah did not speak to her.

Once, during the night, Sarah woke up; she sat up in bed and stared into the darkness. Then she smiled to herself. As she lay down again she thought:

"Now I know that she will bring it."

The next day was very fine, and in the glittering garden by the fountain, Sarah sat with Hortense, and waited. Soon Mary and her nurse appeared. Sarah took Mary by the hand and they went away down the leaf-strewn path.

"Well!" said Sarah.

Mary quite silently felt in her pocket at the back of her short, green frock, produced the ring, gave it to Sarah, and, still without a word, turned back down the path and walked to her nurse. She stood there, clutching a doll in her hand, stared in front of her, and said nothing. Sarah looked at the ring, smiled, and put it into her pocket.

At that instant the climax of the whole affair struck, like a blow from some one unseen, upon Sarah's consciousness. She should have been triumphant. She was not. Her one thought as she looked at the ring was that she wished Mary had not taken it. She had a strange feeling as though Mary, soft and heavy and fat, were hanging round her neck. She had "got" Mary for ever. She was suddenly conscious that she despised Mary, and had lost all interest in her. She didn't want the ring, nor did she ever wish to see Mary again.

She gazed about the garden, shrugged her thin, little, bony shoulders as though she were fifty at least, and felt tired and dull, as on the day after a party. She stood and looked at Mary and her nurse; when she saw them walk away she did not move, but stayed there, staring after them. She was greatly disappointed; she did not feel any pleasure at having forced Mary to obey her, but would have liked to have smacked and bitten her, could these violent actions have driven her into speech. In some undetermined way Mary's silence had beaten Sarah. Mary was a stupid, silly little girl, and Sarah despised and scorned her, but, somehow, that was not enough; from all of this, it simply remained that Sarah would like now to forget her, and could not. What did the silly little thing mean by looking like that? "She'll go and hug her Alice and cry over it." If only she had cried in front of Sarah that would have been something.

Two days later Lady Charlotte was explaining to Sarah that so acute a financial crisis had arrived "as likely as not we shan't have a roof over our heads in a day or two."

"We'll take an organ and a monkey," said Sarah.

"At any rate," Lady Charlotte said, "when you grow up you'll be used to anything."

Mrs. Kitson, untidy, in dishevelled clothing, and great distress, was shown in.

"Dear Lady Charlotte, I must apologise—this absurd hour—but I—we—very unhappy about poor Mary. We can't think what's the matter with her. She's not slept for two nights—in a high fever, and cries and cries. The Doctor—Dr. Williamson —*really* clever—says she's unhappy about some-thing. We thought—scarlet fever—no spots—can't think—perhaps your little girl."

"Poor Mrs. Kitson. How tiresome for you. Do sit down. Perhaps Sarah—"

Sarah shook her head.

"She didn't say she'd a headache in the garden the other day."

Mrs. Kitson gazed appealingly at the little black figure in front of her.

"Do try and remember, dear. Perhaps she told you something."

"Nothing" said Sarah.

"She cries and cries," said Mrs. Kitson, about whose person little white strings and tapes seemed to be continually appearing and disappearing.

"Perhaps she's eaten something?" suggested Lady Charlotte.

When Mrs. Kitson had departed, Lady Charlotte turned to Sarah.

"What have you done to the poor child?" she said.

"Nothing," said Sarah. "I never want to see her again."

"Then you *have* done something?" said Lady Charlotte.

"She's always crying," said Sarah, "and she calls her kitten Alice," as though that were explanation sufficient.

The strange truth remains, however, that the night that followed this conversation was the first unpleasant one that Sarah had ever spent; she remained awake during a great part of it. It was as though the hours that she had spent on that other afternoon, compelling, from her own dark room, Mary's will, had attached Mary to her. Mary was there with her now, in her bedroom. Mary, red-nosed, sniffing, her eyes wide and staring.

"I want to go home."

"Silly little thing," thought Sarah. "I wish I'd never played with her."

In the morning Sarah was tired and white-faced. She would speak to no one. After luncheon she found her hat and coat for herself, let herself out of the house, and walked to Mrs. Kitson's, and was shown into the wide, untidy drawing-room, where books and flowers and papers had a lost and strayed air as though a violent wind had blown through the place and disturbed everything.

Mrs. Kitson came in.

"*You*, dear?" she said.

Sarah looked at the room and then at Mrs. Kitson. Her eyes said: "*What* a place! *What* a woman! *What* a fool!"

"Yes, I've come to explain about Mary."

"About Mary?"

"Yes. It's my fault that she's ill. I took a ring out of that little table there—the gold ring with the red stone—and I made her promise not to tell. It's because she thinks she ought to tell that she's ill."

"*You* took it? *You* stole it?" Before Mrs. Kitson's simple mind an awful picture was now revealed. Here, in this little girl, whom she had preferred as a companion for her beloved Mary, was a thief, a liar, and one, as she could instantly perceive, without shame.

"You *stole* it!"

"Yes; here it is." Sarah laid the ring on the table.

Mrs. Kitson gazed at her with horror, dismay, and even fear.

"Why? Why? Don't you know how wrong it is to take things that don't belong to you?"

"Oh, all that!" said Sarah, waving her hand scornfully. "'I don't want the silly thing, and I don't suppose I'd have kept it, anyhow. I don't know why I've told you," she added. "But I just don't want to be bothered with Mary any more."

"Indeed, you won't be, you wicked girl," said Mrs. Kitson. "To think that I—my grand-father's—I'd never missed it. And you haven't even said you're sorry."

"I'm not," said Sarah quietly. "If Mary wasn't so tiresome and silly those sort of things wouldn't happen. She *makes* me—"

Mrs. Kitson's horror deprived her of all speech, so Sarah, after one more glance of amused cynicism about the room, retired.

As she crossed the Square she knew, with happy relief, that she was free of Mary, that she need never bother about her again. Would *all* the people whom she compelled to obey her hang round her with all their stupidities afterwards? If so, life was not going to be so entertaining as she had hoped. In her dark little brain already was the perception of the trouble that good and stupid souls can cause to bold and reckless ones. She would never bother with any one so feeble as Mary again, but, unless she did, how was she ever to have any fun again?

Then as she climbed the stairs to her room, she was aware of something else.

"I've caught you, after all. You *have* been soft. You've yielded to your better nature. Try as you may you can't get right away from it. Now you'll have to reckon with me more than ever. You see you're not stronger than I am."

Before she opened the door of her room she knew that she would find Him there, triumphant.

With a gesture of impatient irritation she pushed the door open.

CHAPTER IX

YOUNG JOHN SCARLETT

I

That fatal September—the September that was to see young John take his adventurous way to his first private school—surely, steadily approached.

Mrs. Scarlett, an emotional and sentimental little woman, vibrating and taut like a telegraph wire, told herself repeatedly that she would make no sign. The preparations proceeded, the date—September 23rd—was constantly evoked, a dreadful ghost, by the careless, light-hearted family. Mr. Scarlett made no sign.

From the hour of John's birth—nearly ten years ago—Mrs. Scarlett had never known a day when she had not been compelled to control her sentimental affections. From the first John had been an adorable baby, from the first he had followed his father in the rejection of all sentiment as un-English, and even if larger questions are involved, unpatriotic, but also from the first he had hinted, in surprising, furtive, agitating moments, at poetry, imagination, hidden, romantic secrets. Tom, May, Clare, the older children, had never been known to hint at anything—hints were not at all in their line, and of imagination they had not, between them, enough to fill a silver thimble—they were good, sturdy, honest children, with healthy stomachs and an excellent determination to do exactly the things that their class and generation were bent upon doing. Mrs. Scarlett was fond of them, of course, and because she was a sentimental woman she was sometimes quite needlessly emotional about them, but John—no. John was of another world.

The other children felt, beyond question, this difference. They deferred to John about everything and regarded him as leader of the family, and in their deference there was more than simply a recognition of his sturdy independence. Even John's father, Mr. Reginald Scarlett, a K.C., and a man of a most decisive and emphatic bearing, felt John's difference.

John's appearance was unengaging rather than handsome—a snub nose, grey eyes, rather large ears, a square, stocky body and short, stout legs. He was certainly the most independent small boy in England, and very obstinate; when any proposal that seemed on the face of it absurd was made to him, he shut up like a box. His mouth would close, his eyes disappear, all light and colour would die from his face, and it was as though he said: "Well, if you are stupid enough to persist in this thing you can compel me, of course—you are physically stronger than I—but you will only get me like this quite dead and useless, and a lot of good may it do you!"

There were times, of course, when he could be most engagingly pleasant. He was courteous, on occasion, with all the beautiful manners that, we are told, are yielding so sadly before the spread of education and the speed of motor-cars— you never could foretell the guest that he would prefer, and it was nothing to him that here was an aunt, an uncle, or a grandfather who must be placated, and there an uninvited, undesired caller who mattered nothing at all. Mr. Scarlett's father he offended mortally by expressing, in front of him, dislike for hair that grew in bushy profusion out of that old gentleman's ears.

"But you could cut it off," he argued, in a voice thick with surprised disgust. His grandfather, who was a baronet, and very wealthy, predicted a dismal career for his grandchild.

All the family realised quite definitely that nothing could be done with John. It was fortunate, indeed, that he was, on the whole, of a happy and friendly disposition. He liked the world and things that he found in it. He liked games, and food, and adventure—he liked quite tolerably his family—he liked immensely the prospect of going to school.

There were other things—strange, uncertain things—that lay like the dim, uncertain pattern of some tapestry in the back of his mind. He gave *them*, as the months passed, less and less heed. Only sometimes when he was asleep....

Meanwhile, his mother, with the heroism worthy of Boadicea, that great and savage warrior, kept his impulses of devotion, of sacrifice, of adoration, in her heart. John had no need of them; very long ago, Reginald Scarlett, then no K.C., with all the K.C. manner, had told her that *he* did not need them either. She gave her dinner parties, her receptions, her political gatherings—tremulous and smiling she faced a world that thought her a wise, capable little woman, who would see her husband a judge and peer one of these days.

"Mrs. Scarlett—a woman of great social ambition," was their definition of her.

"Mrs. Scarlett—the mother of John," was her own.

II

On a certain night, early in the month of September, young John dreamt again—but for the first time for many months— the dream that had, in the old days, come to him so often. In those days, perhaps, he had not called it a dream. He had not given it a name, and in the quiet early days he had simply greeted, first a protector, then a friend. But that was all very long ago, when one was a baby and allowed oneself to imagine anything. He had, of course, grown ashamed of such confiding fancies, and as he had become more confident had shoved away, with stout, determined fingers, those dim memories, poignancies, regrets. How childish one had been at four, and five, and six! How independent and strong now, on the very edge of the world of school! It perturbed him, therefore, that at this moment of crisis this old dream should recur, and it perturbed him the more, as he lay in bed next morning and thought it over, that it should have seemed to him at the time no dream at all, but simply a natural and actual occurrence.

He had been asleep, and then he had been awake. He had seen, sitting on his bed and looking at him with mild, kind eyes his old Friend. His Friend was always the same, conveying so absolutely kindness and protection, and his beard, his hands, the appealing humour of his gaze, recalled to John the early years, with a swift, imperative urgency. John, so independent and assured, felt, nevertheless, again that old alarm of a strange, unreal world, and the necessity of an appeal for protection from the only one of them all who understood.

"Hallo!" said John.

"Well?" said his Friend. "It's many months since I've been to see you, isn't it?"

"That's not my fault,' said John.

"In a way, it is. You haven't wanted me, have you? Haven't given me a thought."

"There's been so much to do. I'm going to school, you know."

"Of course. That's why I have come now."

Beside the window a dark curtain blew forward a little, bulged as though some one were behind it, thinned again in the pale dim shadows of a moon that, beyond the window, fought with driving clouds. That curtain would—how many ages ago!—have tightened young John's heart with terror, and the contrast made by his present slim indifference drew him, in some warm, confiding fashion, closer to his visitor.

"Anyway, I'm jolly glad you've come now. I haven't really forgotten you, ever. Only in the day-time—"

"Oh, yes, you have," his Friend said, smiling. "It's natural enough and right that you should. But if only you will believe always that I once was here, if only you'll not be persuaded into thinking me impossible, silly, absurd, sentimental—with ever so many other things—that's all I've come now to ask you."

"Why, how should I ever?" John demanded indignantly.

"After all, I *was* a help—for a long time when things were difficult and you had so much to learn—all that time you wanted me, and I was here."

"Of course," said John politely, but feeling within him that warning of approaching sentiment that he had learnt by now so fundamentally to dread.

Very well his friend understood his apprehension.

"That's all. I've only come to you now to ask you to make me a promise—a very easy one."

"Yes?" said John.

"It's only that when you go off to school—before you leave this house—you will just, for a moment, remember me just then, and say good-bye to me. We've been a lot here in these rooms, in these passages, up and down together, and if only, as you go, you'll think of me, I'll be there.... Every year you've thought of me less—that doesn't matter—but it matters more than you know that you should remember me just for an instant, just to say good-bye. Will you promise me?"

"Why, of course," said John.

"Don't forget! Don't forget! Don't forget!" And the kindly shadow had faded, the voice lingering about the room, mingling with the faint silver moonlight, passing out into the wider spaciousness of the rolling clouds.

III

With the clear light of morning came the confident certainty that it had all been the merest dream, and yet that certainty did not sweep the affair, as it should have done, from young John's brain and heart. He was puzzled, perplexed, disturbed, unhappy. The "twenty-third" was approaching with terrible rapidity, and it was essential now that he should summon to aid all the forces of manly self-control and common-sense. And yet, just at this time, of all others, came that disturbing dream and, in its train, absurd memories and fancies, burdened, too, with an urgent prompting of gratitude to some one or something. He shook it off, he obstinately rebelled, but he dreaded the night, and, with a sigh of relief, hailed the morning that followed a dreamless sleep.

Worst of all, he caught himself yielding to thoughts like these: "But he was kind to me—awfully decent" (a phrase caught from his elder brother). "I remember how He ..." And then he would shake himself. "It was only a silly old dream. He wasn't real a bit. I'm not a rotten kid now that thinks fairies and all that true."

He was bothered, too, by the affectionate sentiment (still disguised, but ever, as the days proceeded, more thinly) of his mother and sisters. The girls, May and Clare, adored young John. His elder brother was away with a school friend. John, therefore, was left to feminine attention, and very tiresome he found it. May and Clare, girls of no imagination, saw only the drama that they might extract for themselves out of the affair. They knew what school was like, especially at first—John was going to be utterly wretched, miserably homesick, bullied, kept in over horrible sums and impossible Latin exercises, ill-fed, and trodden upon at games. They did not really believe these things—they knew that their brother, Tom, had always had a most pleasant time, and John was precisely the type of boy who would prosper at school, but they indulged, just for this fortnight, their romantic sentiment, never alluded in speech to school and its terrors, but by their pitying avoidance of the subject filled the atmosphere with their agitation. They were working things for John—May, handkerchiefs, and Clare, a comforter; their voices were soft and charged with omens, their eyes were bright with the drama of the event, as though they had been supporting some young Christian relation before his encounter with the lions. John hated more and more and more.

But more terrible to him than his sisters was his mother. He was too young to understand what his departure meant to her, but he knew that there was something real here that needed comforting. He wanted to comfort her, and yet hated the atmosphere of emotion that he felt in himself as well as in her. They ought to know, he argued, that the least little thing would make him break down like an ass and behave as no man should, and yet they were doing everything.... Oh, if only Tom were here! Then, at any rate, would be brutal common-sense. There were special meals for him during this fortnight, and an eager inviting of his opinion as to how the days should be spent. On the last night of all they were to go to the theatre—a real play this time, none of your pantomime!

There was, moreover, all the business of clothes—fine, rich, stiff new garments—a new Eton jacket, a round black coat, a shining bowler-hat, new boots. He watched this stir with a brave assumption that he had been surveying it all his life, but a horrible tight pain in the bottom of his throat told him that he was a bravado, almost a liar.

He found himself, now that the "twenty-third" was gaping right there in front of him, with its fiery throat wide and flaming, doing the strangest thing. He was frightened of the dusk, he would run through the passage and up the stairs at breathless speed, he would look for a moment at the lamp-lit square with the lights of the opposite houses tigers' eyes, and the trees filmy like smoke, then would hastily draw the curtains and greet the warm inhabited room with a little gasp of reassurance. Strangest of all, he found himself often in the old nursery at the top of the house. Very seldom did any one come there now, and it had the pathos of a room grown cold and comfortless. Most of the toys were put away or given to hospitals, but the rocking-horse with his Christmas-tree tail was there, and the doll's-house, and a railway with trains and stations.

He was here. He was saying to himself: "Yes, it was just over there, by the window, that He came that time. He talked to me there. That other time it was when I was down by the doll's-house. He showed me the smoke coming up from the chimneys when the sun stuck through, and the moon was all red one night, and the stars."

He found himself gazing out over the square, over the twisted chimneys, that seemed to be laughing at him, over the shining wires and glittering roofs, out to the mist that wrapped the city beyond his vision—so vast, so huge, so many people—March Square was nothing. He was nothing—John Scarlett nothing at all.

Then, with a sigh, he turned back. His Friend, the other night, had been real enough. Fairies, ghosts, goblins and dragons— everything was real. Everything. It was all terrible, terrible to think of, but, above and beyond all else, he must not forget, on the day of his departure, that farewell; something disastrous would come upon him were he so ungrateful.

And then he would go downstairs again, down to newspapers and fires, toast and tea, the large print of Frith's "Railway Station," and the coloured supplement of Greiffenhagen's "Idyll," and the tattered numbers of the *Windsor* and the

Strand magazines, and, behold, all these things were real and all the things in the nursery unreal. Could it be that both worlds were real? Even now, at his tender years, that old business of connecting the Dream and the Business was at his throat.

"Teal Tea! Tea!" Frantic screams from May. "There's some new jam, and, John, mother says she wants you to try on some underclothes afterwards. Those others didn't do, she said...."

There came then the disastrous hour—an hour that John was never, in all his after-life, to forget. On a wild stormy evening he found himself in the nursery. A week remained now—to-day fortnight he would be in another world, an alarming, fierce, tremendous world. He looked at the rocking-horse with its absurd tail and the patch on its back, that had been worn away by its faithful riders, and suddenly he was crying. This was a thing that he never did, that he had strenuously, persistently refrained from doing all these weeks, but now, in the strangest way, it was the conviction that the world into which he was going wouldn't care in the least for the doll's-house, and would mock brutally, derisively at the rocking-horse, that defeated him. It was even the knowledge that, in a very short time, he himself would be mocking.

He sat down on the floor and cried. The door opened; before he could resist or make any movement, his mother's arms were about him, his mother's cheek against his, and she was whispering: "Oh, my darling, my darling!"

The horrible thing then occurred. He was savage, with a wild, fierce, protesting rage. His cheeks flamed. His tears were instantly dried. That he should have been caught thus! That, when he had been presenting so brave and callous a front to the world, at the one weak and shameful moment he should have been discovered! He scarcely realised that this was his mother, he did not care who it was. It was as though he had been delivered into the most horrible and shameful of traps. He pushed her from him; he struggled fiercely on his feet. He regarded her with fiery eyes.

"It isn't—I wasn't—you oughtn't to have come in. You needn't imagine—"

He burst from the room. A shameful, horrible experience.

But it cannot be denied that he was ashamed afterwards. He loved his mother, whereas he merely liked the rest of the family. He would not hurt her for worlds, and yet, why *must* she—

And strangely, mysteriously, her attitude was confused in his mind with his dreams, and his Friend, and the red moon, and the comic chimneys.

He knew, however, that, during this last week he must be especially nice to his mother, and, with an elaborate courtesy and strained attention, he did his best.

The last night arrived, and, very smart and excited, they went to the theatre. The boxes had been packed, and stood in a shining and self-conscious trio in John's bedroom. The new play-box was there, with its stolid freshness and the black bands at the corners; inside, there was a multitude of riches, and it was, of course, a symbol of absolute independence and maturity. John was wearing the new Eton jacket, also a new white waistcoat; the parting in his hair was straighter than it had ever been before, his ears were pink. The world seemed a confused mixture of soap and starch and lights. Piccadilly Circus was a cauldron of bubbling colour.

His breath came in little gasps, but his face, with its snub nose and large mouth, was grave and composed; up and down his back little shivers were running. When the car stopped outside the theatre he gave a little gulp. His father, who was, for once, moved by the occasion, said an idiotic thing;

"Excited, my son?"

With his head high he walked ahead of them, trod on a lady's dress, blushed, heard his father say: "Look where you're going, my boy," heard May giggle, frowned indignantly, and was conscious of the horrid pressure of his collar-stud against his throat; arrived, hot, confused, and very proud, in the dark splendour of the box.

The first play of his life, and how magnificent a play it was! It might have been a rotten affair with endless conversations—luckily there were no discussions at all. All the characters either loved or hated one another too deeply to waste time in talk. They were Roundheads and Cavaliers, and a splendid hero, who had once been a bad fellow, but was now sorry, fought nine Roundheads at once, and was tortured "off" with red lights and his lady waiting for results before a sympathetic audience.

During the torture scene John's heart stopped entirely, his brow was damp, his hand sought his mother's, found it, and held it very hard. She, as she felt his hot fingers pressing against hers, began to see the stage through a mist of tears. She had behaved very well during the past weeks, but the soul that she adored was, to-morrow morning, to be hurled out, wildly, helter-skelter, to receive such tarnishing as it might please Fate to think good.

"I *can't* let him go! I *can't* let him go!"

The curtain came down.

John turned, his eyes wide, his cheeks pale with a pink spot on the middle of each.

"I say, pass those chocolates along!" he whispered hoarsely. Then, recovering himself a little: "I wonder what they did to him? They *must* have done something to his legs, because they were all crooked when he came out."

EPILOGUE

HUGH SEYMOUR

I

It happened that Hugh Seymour, in the month of December, 1911, found himself in the dreamy orchard-bound cathedral city of Polchester. Polchester, as all its inhabitants well know, is famous for its cathedral, its buns, and its river, the cathedral being one of the oldest, the buns being among the sweetest, and the Pol being amongst the most beautiful of the cathedrals, buns and rivers of Great Britain.

Seymour had known Polchester since he was five years old, when he first lived there with his father and mother, but he had only once during the last ten years been able to visit Glebeshire, and then he had been to Rafiel, a fishing village on the south coast. He had, therefore, not seen Polchester since his childhood, and now it seemed to him to have shrivelled from a world of infinite space and mystery into a toy town that would be soon packed away in a box and hidden in a cupboard. As he walked up and down the cobbled streets he was moved by a great affection and sentiment for it. As he climbed the hill to the cathedral, as he stood inside the Close with its lawns, its elm trees, its crooked cobbled walks, its gardens, its houses with old bow windows and deep overhanging doors, he was again a very small boy with soap in his eyes, a shining white collar tight about his neck, and his Eton jacket stiff and unfriendly. He was walking up the aisle with his mother, his boots creaked, the bell's note was dropping, dropping, the fat verger with his staff was undoing the cord of their seat, the boys of the choir-school were looking at him and he was blushing, he was on his knees and the edge of the kneeler was cutting into his trousers, the precentor's voice, as remote from things human as the cathedral bell itself, was crying, "Dearly beloved brethren." He would stop there and wonder whether there could be any connection between that time and this, whether those things had really happened to him, whether he might now be dreaming and would wake up presently to find that it would be soon time to start for the cathedral, that if he and his sisters were good they would have a chapter of the "Pillars of the House" read to them after tea, with one chocolate each at the end of every two pages. No, he was real, March Square was real, Polchester was real, Glebeshire and London were real together—nothing died, nothing passed away.

On the second afternoon of his stay he was standing in the Close, bathed now in yellow sunlight, when he saw coming towards him a familiar figure. One glance was enough to assure him that this was the Rev. William Lasher, once Vicar of Clinton St. Mary, now Canon of Polchester Cathedral. Mr. Lasher it was, and Mr. Lasher the same as he had ever been. He was walking with his old energetic stride, his head up, his black overcoat flapping behind him, his eyes sharply investigating in and out and all round him. He saw Seymour, but did not recognise him, and would have passed on.

"You don't know me?" said Seymour, holding out his hand.

"I beg your pardon, I—" said Canon Lasher.

"Seymour—Hugh Seymour—whom you were once kind enough to look after at Clinton St. Mary."

"Why! Fancy! Indeed. My dear boy. My dear boy!" Mr. Lasher was immensely cordial in exactly his old, healthy, direct manner. He insisted that Seymour should come with him and drink a cup of tea. Mrs. Lasher would be delighted. They had often wondered.... Only the other day Mrs. Lasher was saying.... "And you're one of our novelists, I hear," said Canon Lasher in exactly the tone that he would have used had Seymour taken to tight-rope walking at the Halls.

"Oh, no!" said Seymour, laughing, "that's another man of my name. I'm at the Bar."

"Ah," said the Canon, greatly relieved, "that's good! That's good! Very good indeed!"

Mrs. Lasher was, of course, immensely surprised. "Why! Fancy! And it was only yesterday! Whoever would have expected! I never was more astonished! And tea just ready! How fortunate! Just fancy you meeting the Canon!"

The Canon seemed, to Seymour, greatly mellowed by comfort and prosperity; there was even the possibility of corpulence in the not distant future. He was, indeed, a proper Canon.

"And who," said Seymour, "has Clinton St. Mary now?"

"One of the Trenchards," said Mr. Lasher. "As you know, a very famous old Glebeshire family. There are some younger cousins of the Garth Trenchards, I believe. You know of the Trenchards of Garth? No? Ah, very delightful people. You should know them. Yes, Jim Trenchard, the man at Clinton, is a few years senior to myself. He was priest when I was deacon in—let me see—dear me, how the years fly—in—'pon my word, how time goes!"

All of which gave Seymour to understand that the Rev. James Trenchard was a failure in life, although a good enough fellow. Then it was that suddenly, in the heart of that warm and cosy drawing-room, Hugh Seymour was, sharply, as though by a douche of cold water, awakened to the fact that he must see Clinton St. Mary again. It appeared to him, now, with its lanes, its hedges, the village green, the moor, the Borhaze

Road, the pirates, yes, and the Scarecrow. It came there, across the Canon's sumptuous Turkey carpet, and demanded his presence.

"I must go," Seymour said, getting up and speaking in a strange, bewildered voice as though he were just awakening from a dream. He left them, at last, promising to come and see them again.

He heard the Canon's voice in his ears: "Always a knife and fork, my boy ... any time if you let us know." He stepped down into the little lighted streets, into the town with its cosy security and some scent, even then in the heart of winter, perhaps, from the fruit of its many orchards. The moon, once again an orange feather in the sky, reminded him of those early days that seemed now to be streaming in upon him from every side.

Early next morning he caught the ten o'clock train to Clinton.

II

"Why," in the train he continued to say to himself, "have I let all these years pass without returning? Why have I never returned?... Why have I never returned?"

The slow, sleepy train (the London express never stops at Clinton) jerked through the deep valleys, heavy with woods, golden brown at their heart, the low hills carrying, on their horizons, white drifting clouds that flung long grey shadows. Seymour felt suddenly as though he could never return to London again exactly as he had returned to it before. "That period of my life is over, quite over.... Some one is taking me down here now—I know that I am being compelled to go. But I want to go. I am happier than I have ever been in my life before."

Often, in Glebeshire, December days are warm and mellow

like the early days of September. It so was now; the country was wrapped in with happy content, birds rose and hung, like telegraph wires, beyond the windows. On a slanting brown field gulls from the sea, white and shining, were hovering, wheeling, sinking into the soil. And yet, as he went, he was not leaving March Square behind, but rather taking it with him He was taking the children too—Bim, Angelina, John, even Sarah (against her will), and it was not her who was in charge of the party. He felt as though, the railway carriages were full and he ought to say continually, "Now, Bim, be quiet. Sit still and look at the picture-book I gave you. Sarah, I shall leave you at the next station if you aren't careful," and that she replied, giving him one of her dark sarcastic looks, "I don't care if you do. I know how to get home all right without your help."

He wished that he hadn't brought her, and yet he couldn't help himself. They all had to come. Then, as he looked about the empty carriage, he laughed at himself. Only a fat farmer reading *The Glebeshire Times*.

"Marnin', sir," said the farmer. "Warm Christmas we'll be havin', I reckon. Yes, indeed. I see the Bishop's dying—poor old soul too."

When they arrived at Clinton he caught himself turning round as though to collect his charges; he thought that the farmer looked at him curiously.

"Coming back again has turned my wits.... Now, Angelina, hurry up, can't wait all day." He stopped then abruptly, to pull himself together. "Look here, you're alone, and if you think you're not, you're mad. Remember that you're at the Bar and not even a novelist, so that you have no excuse."

The little platform—usually swept by all the winds of the sea, but now as warm as a toasted bun—flooded him with memory. It was a platform especially connected with school, with departure and return—departures when money in one's pocket and cake in one's play-box did not compensate for the hot pain in one's throat and the cold marble feeling of one's legs; but when every feeling of every sort was swallowed by the great overwhelming desire that the train would go so that one need not any longer be agonised by the efforts of replying to Mr. Lasher's continued last words: "Well, good-bye, my boy. A good time, both at work and play"—the train was off.

"Ticket, please, sir!" said the long-legged young man at the little wooden gate. Seymour plunged down into the deep, high-hedged lane that even now, in winter, seemed to cover him with a fragrant odour of green leaves, of flowers, of wet soil, of sea spray. He was now so conscious of his company that the knowledge of it could not be avoided. It seemed to him that he heard them chattering together, knew that behind his back Sarah was trying to whisper horrid things in Bim's ear, and that he was laughing at her, which made her furious.

"I must have eaten something," he thought. "It's the strangest feeling I've ever had. I just won't take any notice of them. I'll go on as though they weren't there." But the strangest thing of all was that he felt as though he himself were being taken. He had the most comfortable feeling that there was no need for him to give any thought or any kind of trouble. "You just leave it all to me," some one said to him. "I've made all the arrangements."

The lane was hot, and the midday winter sun covered the paths with pools and splashes of colour. He came out on to the common and saw the village, the long straggling street with the white-washed cottages and the hideous grey-slate roofs; the church tower, rising out of the elms, and the pond, running to the common's edge, its water chequered with the reflection of the white clouds above it.

The main street of Clinton is not a lovely street; the inland villages and towns of Glebeshire are, unless you love them, amongst the ugliest things in England, but every step caught at Seymour's heart.

Hugh Walpole

There was Mr. Roscoe's shop which was also the post-office, and in its window was the same collection of liquorice sticks, saffron buns, reels of cotton, a coloured picture of the royal family, views of Trezent Head, Borhaze Beach, St. Arthe Church, cotton blouses made apparently for dolls, so minute were they, three books, "Ben Hur," "The Wide, Wide World," and "St. Elmo," two bottles of sweets, some eau-de-Cologne, and a large white card with bone buttons on it. So moving was this collection to Seymour that he stared at the window as though he were in a trance.

The arrangement of the articles was exactly the same as it had been in the earlier days—the royal family in the middle, supported by the jars of sweets; the three books, very dusty and faded, in the very front; and the bootlaces and liquorice sticks all mixed together as though Mr. Roscoe had forgotten which was which.

"Look here, Bim," he said aloud, "I've left you up—I really am going off my head!" he thought. He hurried away. "If I *am* mad I'm awfully happy," he said.

III

The white vicarage gate closed behind him with precisely the old-remembered sound—the whiz, the sudden startled pause, the satisfied click. Seymour stood on the sun-bathed lawn, glittering now like green glass, and stared at the house. Its square front of faded red brick preserved a tranquil silence; the only sound in the place was the movement of some birds, his old friend the robin perhaps in the laurel bushes behind him

Although the sun was so warm there was in the air a foreshadowing of a frosty night; and some Christmas roses, smiling at him from the flower beds to right and left of the hall door, seemed to him that they remembered him; but, indeed, the whole house seemed to tell him that. There it waited for him, so silent, laid ready for his acceptance under the blue sky and with no breath of wind stirring. So beautiful was the silence, that he made a movement with his hand as though to tell his companion to be quiet. He felt that they were crowded in an interested, amused group behind him waiting to see what he would do. Then a little bell rang somewhere in the house, a voice cried "Martha!"

He moved forward and pulled the wire of the bell; there was a wheezy jangle, a pause, and then a sharp irritated sound far away in the heart of the house, as though he had hit it in the wind and it protested. An old woman, very neat (she was certainly a Glebeshire woman), told him that Mr. Trenchard was at home. She took him through the dark passages into the study that he knew so well, and said that Mr. Trenchard would be with him in a moment.

It was the same study, and yet how different! Many of the old pieces of furniture were there—the deep, worn leather arm-chair in which Mr. Lasher had been sitting when he had his famous discussion with Mr. Pidgen, the same bookshelves, the same tiles in the fireplace with Bible pictures painted on them, the same huge black coal-scuttle, the same long, dark writing-table. But instead of the old order and discipline there was now a confusion that gave the room the air of a waste-paper basket. Books were piled, up and down, in the shelves, they dribbled on to the floor and lay in little trickling streams across the carpet; old bundles of papers, yellow with age, tied with string and faded blue tape, were in heaps upon the window-sill, and in tumbling cascades in the very middle of the floor; the writing-table itself was so hopelessly littered with books, sermon papers, old letters and new letters, bottles of ink, bottles of glue, three huge volumes of a Bible Concordance, photographs, and sticks of sealing-wax, that the man who could be happy amid such confusion must surely be a kindly and benevolent creature. How orderly had been Mr. Lasher's table, with all the pens in rows, and little sharp drawers that clicked, marked A, B, and C, to put papers into.

Mr. Trenchard entered.

He was what the room had prophesied—fat, red-faced, bald, extremely untidy, with stains on his coat and tobacco on his coat, that was turning a little green, and chalk on his trousers. His eyes shone with pleased friendliness, but there was a little pucker in his forehead, as though his life had not always been pleasant. He rubbed his nose, as he talked, with the back of his hand, and made sudden little darts at the chalk on his trousers, as though he would brush it off. He had the face of an innocent baby, and when he spoke he looked at his companion with exactly the gaze of trusting confidence that a child bestows upon its elders.

"I hope you will forgive me," said Seymour, smiling; "I've come, too, at such an awkward time, but the truth is I simply couldn't help myself. I ought, besides, to catch the four o'clock train back to Polchester."

"Yes, indeed," said Mr. Trenchard, smiling, rubbing his hands together, and altogether in the dark as to what his visitor might be wanting.

"Ah, but I haven't explained; how stupid of me! My name is Seymour. I was here during several years, as a small boy, with Canon Lasher—in my holidays, you know. It's years ago, and I've never been back. I was at Polchester this morning and suddenly felt that I must come over. I wondered whether you'd be so good as to let me look a little at the house and garden."

There was nothing that Mr. Trenchard would like better. How was Canon Lasher? Well? Good. They met sometimes at meetings at Polchester. Canon Lasher, Mr. Trenchard believed, liked it better at Polchester than at Clinton. Honestly, it would break Mr. Trenchard's heart if *he* had to leave the place. But there was no danger of that now. Would Mr. Seymour—his wife would be delighted—would he stay to luncheon?

"Why, that is too kind of you," said Seymour, hesitating, "but there are so many of us, such a lot—I mean," he said hurriedly, at Mr. Trenchard's innocent stare of surprise, "that it's too hard on Mrs. Trenchard, with so little notice."

He broke off confusedly.

"We shall only be too delighted," said Mr. Trenchard. "And if you have friends ..."

"No, no," said Seymour, "I'm quite alone."

When, afterwards, he was introduced to Mrs. Trenchard in the drawing-room, he liked her at once. She was a little woman, very neat, with grey hair brushed back from her forehead. She was like some fresh, mild-coloured fruit, and an old-fashioned dress of rather faded green silk, and a large locket that she wore gave her a settled, tranquil air as though she had always been the same, and would continue so for many years. She had a high, fresh colour, a beautiful complexion and her hands had the delicacy of fragile egg-shell china. She was cheerful and friendly, but was, nevertheless, a sad woman; her eyes were dark and her voice was a little forced as though she had accustomed herself to be in good spirits. The love between herself and her husband was very pleasant to see.

Like all simple people, they immediately trusted Seymour with their confidence. During luncheon they told him many things, of Rasselas, where Mr. Trenchard had been a curate, at their joy at getting the Clinton living, and of their happiness at being there, of the kindness of the people, of the beauty of the country, of their neighbours, of their relations, the George Trenchards, at Garth of Glebeshire generally, and what it meant to be a Trenchard.

"There've been Trenchards in Glebeshire," said the Vicar, greatly excited, "since the beginning of time. If Adam and Eve were here, and Glebeshire was the Garden of Eden, as I daresay it was, why, then Adam was a Trenchard."

Afterwards when they were smoking in the confused study, Seymour learnt why Mrs. Trenchard was a sad woman.

"We've had one trial, under God's grace," said Mr. Trenchard. "There was a boy and a girl—Francis and Jessamy. They died, both, in a bad epidemic of typhoid here, five years ago. Francis was five, Jessamy four. 'The Lord giveth and the Lord taketh away.' It was hard losing both of them. They got ill together and died on the same day."

He puffed furiously at his pipe. "Mrs. Trenchard keeps the nursery just the same as it used to be. She'll show it to you, I daresay."

Later, when Mrs. Trenchard took him over the house, his sight of the nursery was more moving to him than any of his old memories. She unlocked the door with a sharp turn of the wrist and showed him the wide sun-lit room, still with fresh curtains, with a wall-paper of robins and cherries, with the toys—dolls, soldiers, a big dolls'-house, a rocking-horse, boxes of bricks.

"Our two children, who died five years ago," she said in her quiet, calm voice, "this was their room. These were their things. I haven't been able to change it as yet. Mr. Lasher," she said, smiling up at him, "had no children, and you were too old for a nursery, I suppose."

It was then, as he stood in the doorway, bathed in a shaft of sunlight, that he was again, with absolute physical consciousness, aware of the children's presence. He could tell that they were pressing behind him, staring past him into the room, he could almost hear their whispered exclamations of delight.

He turned to Mrs. Trenchard as though she must have perceived that he was not alone. But she had noticed nothing; with another sharp turn of the wrist she had locked the door.

IV

To-morrow was Christmas Eve: he had promised to spend

Christmas with friends in Somerset. Now he went to the little village post-office and telegraphed that he was detained; he felt at that moment as though he would never like to leave Clinton again.

The inn, the "Hearty Cow," was kept by people who were new to him—"foreigners, from up-country." The fat landlord complained to Seymour of the slowness of the Clinton people, that they never could be induced to see things to their own proper advantage. "A dead-alive place *I* call it," he said; "but still, mind you," he added, "it's got a sort of a 'old on one."

From the diamond-paned windows of his bedroom next morning he surveyed a glorious day, the very sky seemed to glitter with frost, and when his window was opened he could hear quite plainly the bell on Trezent Rock, so crystal was the air. He walked that morning for miles; he covered all his old ground, picking up memories as though he were building a pleasure-house. Here was his dream, there was disappointment, here that flaming discovery, there this sudden terror— nothing had changed for him, the Moor, St. Arthe Church, St. Dreot Woods, the high white gates and mysterious hidden park of Portcullis House—all were as though it had been yesterday that he had last seen them. Polchester had dwindled before his giant growth. Here the moor, the woods, the roads had grown, and it was he that had shrunken.

At last he stood on the sand-dunes that bounded the moor and looked down upon the marbled sand, blue and gold after the retreating tide. The faint lisp and curdle of the sea sang to him. A row of sea-gulls, one and then another quivering in the light, stood at the water's edge; the stiff grass that pushed its way fiercely from the sand of the dunes was white with hoar-frost, and the moon, silver now, and sharply curved, came climbing behind the hill.

He turned back and went home. He had promised to have tea at the Vicarage, and he found Mrs. Trenchard putting holly over the pictures in the little dark square hall. She looked as though she had always been there, and as though, in some curious way, the holly, with its bright red berries, especially belonged to her.

She asked him to help her, and Seymour thought that he must have known her all his life. She had a tranquil, restful air, but now and then, hummed a little tune. She was very tidy as she moved about, picking up little scraps of holly. A row of pins shone in her green dress. After a while they went upstairs and hung holly in the passages.

Seymour had turned his back to her and was balanced on a little ladder, when he heard her utter a sharp little cry.

"The nursery door's open," she said. He turned, and saw very clearly, against the half-light, her startled eyes. Her hands were pressed against her dress and holly had fallen at her feet. He saw, too, that the nursery door was ajar.

"I locked it myself, yesterday; you saw me."

She gasped as though she had been running, and he saw that her face was white.

He moved forward quickly and pushed open the door. The room itself was lightened by the gleam from the passage and also by the moonlight that came dimly through the window. The shadow of some great tree was flung upon the floor. He saw, at once, that the room was changed. The rocking-horse that had been yesterday against the wall had now been dragged far across the floor. The white front of the dolls'-house had swung open and the furniture was disturbed as though some child had been interrupted in his play. Four large dolls sat solemnly round a dolls' tea-table, and a dolls' tea service was arranged in front of them. In the very centre of the room a fine castle of bricks had been rising, a perfect Tower of Babel in its frustrated ambition.

The shadow of the great tree shook and quivered above

these things.

Seymour saw Mrs. Trenchard's face, he heard her whisper:

"Who is it? What is it?"

Then she fell upon her knees near the tower of bricks. She gazed at them, stared round the rest of the room, then looked up at him, saying very quietly:

"I knew that they would come back one day. I always waited. It must have been they. Only Francis ever built the bricks like that, with the red ones in the middle. He always said they *must* be...."

She broke off and then, with her hands pressed to her face, cried, so softly and so gently that she made scarcely any sound.

Seymour left her.

V

He passed through the house without any one seeing him, crossed the common, and went up to his bedroom at the inn. He sat down before his window with his back to the room. He flung the rattling panes wide.

The room looked out across on to the moor, and he could see, in the moonlight, the faint thread of the beginning of the Borhaze Road. To the left of this there was some sharp point of light, some cottage perhaps. It flashed at him as though it were trying to attract his attention. The night was so magical, the world so wonderful, so without bound or limit, that he was prepared now to wait, passively, for his experience. That point of light was where the Scarecrow used to be, just where the brown fields rise up against the horizon. In all his walks to-day he had deliberately avoided that direction. The Scarecrow would not be there now; he had always in his heart fancied it there, and he would not change that picture that he had of it. But now the light flashed at him. As he stared at it he knew that to-day he had completed that adventure that had begun for him many years ago, on that Christmas Eve when he had met Mr. Pidgen.

They were whispering in his ear, "We've had a lovely day. It was the most beautiful nursery.... Two other children came too. They wore *their* things...."

"What, after all," said his Friend's voice, "does it mean but that if you love enough we are with you everywhere—for ever?"

And then the children's voices again:

"She thought they'd come back, but they'd never gone away—really, you know."

He gazed once more at the point of light, and then turned round and faced the dark room....

ABOUT THE AUTHOR

 **Sir Hugh Seymour Walpole** (March 13, 1884 - June 1, 1941), was an English novelist.

He was born in Auckland in New Zealand and educated in England at the King's School, Canterbury and at Emmanuel College, Cambridge. He worked as a teacher before turning to writing full time. His first novel was The Wooden Horse (1909), with Fortitude (1913) his first great success. He worked for the Red Cross in Russia during World War I, experiences which fed his The Dark Forest (1916) and The Secret City (1919). The latter won the inaugural James Tait Black Memorial Prize.

Walpole lived at Brackenburn Lodge on the slopes of Catbells in the Lake District from 1924 to his death. Here he wrote many of his best known works including the family saga The Herries Chronicle, comprising Rogue Herries (1930), Judith Paris (1931), The Fortress (1932) and Vanessa (1933). Farthing Hall (1929) was produced in collaboration with J.B. Priestley.

Walpole's work was very popular, and brought him great financial rewards. He was a prolific worker who embraced a variety of genres. These included: short stories; school novels (Mr Perrin and Mr Traill, 1911 and the Jeremy trilogy) that delve deep into the psychology of boyhood; gothic horror novels (Portrait of a Man with Red Hair, 1925 and The Killer

& The Slain, 1942); biographies (of Joseph Conrad in 1916, James Branch Cabell in 1920 and Anthony Trollope in 1928); plays and the screenplay for the George Cukor-directed David Copperfield (1935).

He was knighted in 1937. He died while doing volunteer war work in 1941.

Choose from Thousands of 1stWorldLibrary Classics By

A. M. Barnard
Ada Leverson
Adolphus William Ward
Aesop
Agatha Christie
Alexander Aaronsohn
Alexander Kielland
Alexandre Dumas
Alfred Gatty
Alfred Ollivant
Alice Duer Miller
Alice Turner Curtis
Alice Dunbar
Allen Chapman
Alleyne Ireland
Ambrose Bierce
Amelia E. Barr
Amory H. Bradford
Andrew Lang
Andrew McFarland Davis
Andy Adams
Angela Brazil
Anna Alice Chapin
Anna Sewell
Annie Besant
Annie Hamilton Donnell
Annie Payson Call
Annie Roe Carr
Annonaymous
Anton Chekhov
Archibald Lee Fletcher
Arnold Bennett
Arthur C. Benson
Arthur Conan Doyle
Arthur M. Winfield
Arthur Ransome
Arthur Schnitzler
Arthur Train
Atticus
B.H. Baden-Powell
B. M. Bower
B. C. Chatterjee
Baroness Emmuska Orczy
Baroness Orczy
Basil King
Bayard Taylor
Ben Macomber
Bertha Muzzy Bower
Bjornstjerne Bjornson

Booth Tarkington
Boyd Cable
Bram Stoker
C. Collodi
C. E. Orr
C. M. Ingleby
Carolyn Wells
Catherine Parr Traill
Charles A. Eastman
Charles Amory Beach
Charles Dickens
Charles Dudley Warner
Charles Farrar Browne
Charles Ives
Charles Kingsley
Charles Klein
Charles Hanson Towne
Charles Lathrop Pack
Charles Romyn Dake
Charles Whibley
Charles Willing Beale
Charlotte M. Braeme
Charlotte M. Yonge
Charlotte Perkins Stetson
Clair W. Hayes
Clarence Day Jr.
Clarence E. Mulford
Clemence Housman
Confucius
Coningsby Dawson
Cornelis DeWitt Wilcox
Cyril Burleigh
D. H. Lawrence
Daniel Defoe
David Garnett
Dinah Craik
Don Carlos Janes
Donald Keyhoe
Dorothy Kilner
Dougan Clark
Douglas Fairbanks
E. Nesbit
E. P. Roe
E. Phillips Oppenheim
E. S. Brooks
Earl Barnes
Edgar Rice Burroughs
Edith Van Dyne
Edith Wharton

Edward Everett Hale
Edward J. O'Biren
Edward S. Ellis
Edwin L. Arnold
Eleanor Atkins
Eleanor Hallowell Abbott
Eliot Gregory
Elizabeth Gaskell
Elizabeth McCracken
Elizabeth Von Arnim
Ellem Key
Emerson Hough
Emilie F. Carlen
Emily Bronte
Emily Dickinson
Enid Bagnold
Enilor Macartney Lane
Erasmus W. Jones
Ernie Howard Pie
Ethel May Dell
Ethel Turner
Ethel Watts Mumford
Eugene Sue
Eugenie Foa
Eugene Wood
Eustace Hale Ball
Evelyn Everett-green
Everard Cotes
F. H. Cheley
F. J. Cross
F. Marion Crawford
Fannie E. Newberry
Federick Austin Ogg
Ferdinand Ossendowski
Fergus Hume
Florence A. Kilpatrick
Fremont B. Deering
Francis Bacon
Francis Darwin
Frances Hodgson Burnett
Frances Parkinson Keyes
Frank Gee Patchin
Frank Harris
Frank Jewett Mather
Frank L. Packard
Frank V. Webster
Frederic Stewart Isham
Frederick Trevor Hill
Frederick Winslow Taylor

Friedrich Kerst
Friedrich Nietzsche
Fyodor Dostoyevsky
G.A. Henty
G.K. Chesterton
Gabrielle E. Jackson
Garrett P. Serviss
Gaston Leroux
George A. Warren
George Ade
Geroge Bernard Shaw
George Cary Eggleston
George Durston
George Ebers
George Eliot
George Gissing
George MacDonald
George Meredith
George Orwell
George Sylvester Viereck
George Tucker
George W. Cable
George Wharton James
Gertrude Atherton
Gordon Casserly
Grace E. King
Grace Gallatin
Grace Greenwood
Grant Allen
Guillermo A. Sherwell
Gulielma Zollinger
Gustav Flaubert
H. A. Cody
H. B. Irving
H.C. Bailey
H. G. Wells
H. H. Munro
H. Irving Hancock
H. R. Naylor
H. Rider Haggard
H. W. C. Davis
Haldeman Julius
Hall Caine
Hamilton Wright Mabie
Hans Christian Andersen
Harold Avery
Harold McGrath
Harriet Beecher Stowe
Harry Castlemon
Harry Coghill
Harry Houidini

Hayden Carruth
Helent Hunt Jackson
Helen Nicolay
Hendrik Conscience
Hendy David Thoreau
Henri Barbusse
Henrik Ibsen
Henry Adams
Henry Ford
Henry Frost
Henry James
Henry Jones Ford
Henry Seton Merriman
Henry W Longfellow
Herbert A. Giles
Herbert Carter
Herbert N. Casson
Herman Hesse
Hildegard G. Frey
Homer
Honore De Balzac
Horace B. Day
Horace Walpole
Horatio Alger Jr.
Howard Pyle
Howard R. Garis
Hugh Lofting
Hugh Walpole
Humphry Ward
Ian Maclaren
Inez Haynes Gillmore
Irving Bacheller
Isabel Cecilia Williams
Isabel Hornibrook
Israel Abrahams
Ivan Turgenev
J.G.Austin
J. Henri Fabre
J. M. Barrie
J. M. Walsh
J. Macdonald Oxley
J. R. Miller
J. S. Fletcher
J. S. Knowles
J. Storer Clouston
J. W. Duffield
Jack London
Jacob Abbott
James Allen
James Andrews
James Baldwin

James Branch Cabell
James DeMille
James Joyce
James Lane Allen
James Lane Allen
James Oliver Curwood
James Oppenheim
James Otis
James R. Driscoll
Jane Abbott
Jane Austen
Jane L. Stewart
Janet Aldridge
Jens Peter Jacobsen
Jerome K. Jerome
Jessie Graham Flower
John Buchan
John Burroughs
John Cournos
John F. Kennedy
John Gay
John Glasworthy
John Habberton
John Joy Bell
John Kendrick Bangs
John Milton
John Philip Sousa
John Taintor Foote
Jonas Lauritz Idemil Lie
Jonathan Swift
Joseph A. Altsheler
Joseph Carey
Joseph Conrad
Joseph E. Badger Jr
Joseph Hergesheimer
Joseph Jacobs
Jules Vernes
Julian Hawthrone
Julie A Lippmann
Justin Huntly McCarthy
Kakuzo Okakura
Karle Wilson Baker
Kate Chopin
Kenneth Grahame
Kenneth McGaffey
Kate Langley Bosher
Kate Langley Bosher
Katherine Cecil Thurston
Katherine Stokes
L. A. Abbot
L. T. Meade

L. Frank Baum
Latta Griswold
Laura Dent Crane
Laura Lee Hope
Laurence Housman
Lawrence Beasley
Leo Tolstoy
Leonid Andreyev
Lewis Carroll
Lewis Sperry Chafer
Lilian Bell
Lloyd Osbourne
Louis Hughes
Louis Joseph Vance
Louis Tracy
Louisa May Alcott
Lucy Fitch Perkins
Lucy Maud Montgomery
Luther Benson
Lydia Miller Middleton
Lyndon Orr
M. Corvus
M. H. Adams
Margaret E. Sangster
Margret Howth
Margaret Vandercook
Margaret W. Hungerford
Margret Penrose
Maria Edgeworth
Maria Thompson Daviess
Mariano Azuela
Marion Polk Angellotti
Mark Overton
Mark Twain
Mary Austin
Mary Catherine Crowley
Mary Cole
Mary Hastings Bradley
Mary Roberts Rinehart
Mary Rowlandson
M. Wollstonecraft Shelley
Maud Lindsay
Max Beerbohm
Myra Kelly
Nathaniel Hawthrone
Nicolo Machiavelli
O. F. Walton
Oscar Wilde

Owen Johnson
P.G. Wodehouse
Paul and Mabel Thorne
Paul G. Tomlinson
Paul Severing
Percy Brebner
Percy Keese Fitzhugh
Peter B. Kyne
Plato
Quincy Allen
R. Derby Holmes
R. L. Stevenson
R. S. Ball
Rabindranath Tagore
Rahul Alvares
Ralph Bonehill
Ralph Henry Barbour
Ralph Victor
Ralph Waldo Emmerson
Rene Descartes
Ray Cummings
Rex Beach
Rex E. Beach
Richard Harding Davis
Richard Jefferies
Richard Le Gallienne
Robert Barr
Robert Frost
Robert Gordon Anderson
Robert L. Drake
Robert Lansing
Robert Lynd
Robert Michael Ballantyne
Robert W. Chambers
Rosa Nouchette Carey
Rudyard Kipling
Saint Augustine
Samuel B. Allison
Samuel Hopkins Adams
Sarah Bernhardt
Sarah C. Hallowell
Selma Lagerlof
Sherwood Anderson
Sigmund Freud
Standish O'Grady
Stanley Weyman
Stella Benson
Stella M. Francis

Stephen Crane
Stewart Edward White
Stijn Streuvels
Swami Abhedananda
Swami Parmananda
T. S. Ackland
T. S. Arthur
The Princess Der Ling
Thomas A. Janvier
Thomas A Kempis
Thomas Anderton
Thomas Bailey Aldrich
Thomas Bulfinch
Thomas De Quincey
Thomas Dixon
Thomas H. Huxley
Thomas Hardy
Thomas More
Thornton W. Burgess
U. S. Grant
Upton Sinclair
Valentine Williams
Various Authors
Vaughan Kester
Victor Appleton
Victor G. Durham
Victoria Cross
Virginia Woolf
Wadsworth Camp
Walter Camp
Walter Scott
Washington Irving
Wilbur Lawton
Wilkie Collins
Willa Cather
Willard F. Baker
William Dean Howells
William le Queux
W. Makepeace Thackeray
William W. Walter
William Shakespeare
Winston Churchill
Yei Theodora Ozaki
Yogi Ramacharaka
Young E. Allison
Zane Grey